COULSON'S CRUCIBLE

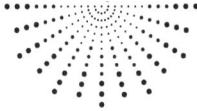

ANNA J. MCINTYRE

Coulson's Crucible
By Anna J. McIntyre

PUBLISHED BY:
Robeth Publishing, LLC
Copyright © 2013 Bobbi Holmes
Copyright © Robeth Publishing, LLC
This is a work of fiction.
Robeth Publishing, LLC
All Rights Reserved.

COULSON FAMILY SAGA
COULSON'S WIFE
COULSON'S CRUCIBLE
COULSON'S LESSONS
COULSON'S SECRET
COULSON'S RECKONING

www.bobbiholmes.com
www.robeth.net
www.annajmcintyreauthor.com

ISBN: 978-1494247416
ISBN: 1494247410

For Mom, my greatest fan and cheerleader.
Thanks for all that you do.

*H*e had finally stopped crying, but she knew he would start again. He always did. Vera made her way up the rear staircase of Coulson House carrying her three-month-old son, who slept soundly in her arms. Someone might see her if she used the main staircase.

No one went to the third floor except for the household staff to clean the unused rooms. Speculation varied as to why her father-in-law had built such an impressive estate. Some said it was for his wife, Mary Ellen, while others insisted it was to show the world he was committed to his project—developing the resort community, which he founded and that bore his name.

Her mother-in-law, Mary Ellen Coulson, had decorated the mansion. Just months after moving into the impressive estate, Mary Ellen had died in its library on the first floor. She was just forty-nine.

Vera wanted to go outside and breathe in the fresh air. Walking into one of the rooms on the third floor, she paid little notice to the ornate furnishings and impressive artwork. Instead, she walked through the room to the French doors leading to the balcony.

It was breezy outside. Vera held the sleeping bundle tighter. She didn't want to wake Russell. Closing her eyes, Vera breathed in the crisp December air, escaping for a moment the prison that was her life. If she could just be free, fly far away from her pain, her sadness. Without thought, she climbed onto the wide banister surrounding the balcony and looked down. It took considerable effort to maintain her balance, especially while holding the sleeping babe.

"Mother!" Vera's eight-year old son, Garret, shouted as he raced through the doorway onto the balcony. His sudden and unexpected appearance caused Vera to lose her balance for a brief moment, but she reached out with her free hand and grabbed the outside of the building to steady herself.

"Please, Mother, get down. You could fall!" Garret begged.

Vera looked down at her son and smiled. "Don't be silly, Garret. I can fly. Come." She reached her hand out to him. "Join me, and I'll show you."

"No, please get down!" Garret began to cry.

"Here, you'll see," Vera said calmly.

Turning away from Garret, she stood precariously atop the banister. Closing her eyes, she prepared to take flight when a gust of air hit the front of her body, sending her sprawling backward onto the balcony floor. The fall woke Russell, who began to cry, but he remained secure in his mother's arms. Garret ran from the balcony.

The abrupt fall knocked the air from Vera's fragile body. Colliding against the balcony floor was painful, yet nothing appeared to be broken. Attempting to catch her breath, she held tight onto the squirming baby. Opening her eyes, Vera looked into the face of Mary Ellen Coulson. Transfixed by the apparition, Vera's eyes widened. The next moment, Mary Ellen was gone.

CHAPTER ONE

*W*ith one little foot in front of the other, she ran faster and faster. Her arms, bent at the elbows, pumped frantically back and forth while the riotous beat of her heart pounded relentlessly. Barely able to catch her breath, she knew they wanted to kill her.

A safe haven was almost within sight, and if she could just reach it in time, she might escape her enemies. Then she saw it and was relieved to find the door was already propped open. There would be no need to pause and take the time to pull open the heavy door and risk capture.

Without missing a beat, Alexandra flew through the open doorway into her sanctuary, kicking the doorstop on her way in, closing the door behind her. She felt a momentary sense of relief. It was short lived, for after she entered the room and looked around, she discovered her protector was not there. To make the situation worse, she was not alone.

Tears filled her hazel eyes as she stared into the frightening face of the stranger. Paralyzed with fear, she stood frozen to the spot and glanced back at the doorway, wondering briefly if it might be possible to escape without encountering the three thugs who vowed revenge.

Looking back to the stranger, who sat quietly in the chair, studying her with serious blue eyes, Alexandra took a deep breath and rallied her courage. "Where's my mommy?" she asked with a quivering voice.

He sat there a moment longer, just staring, before he stood up and walked in her direction—more a swagger than a walk. Taller than many of the other high school boys, he wore faded Levi's and a snug-fitting white T-shirt that accentuated instead of concealed the well-toned muscles of his chest and arms. His short dark hair wasn't as conservative as a crewcut, yet not as brazen as the pompadour.

"Is your mom Mrs. Chamberlain?"

She gave a nod in the affirmative when the door burst open. Three of her brother's classmates rushed in, bent on revenge.

"Hey, baby, your mama's in the office and she ain't gonna help you none!" Andy Smith threatened with a sneer.

Alexandra could no longer hold back the tears. They slid silently down her face, giving testimony to the fact Andy was right; Alexandra was a baby. She hated showing her weakness, yet she didn't regret kicking Andy in the shins earlier, but now it was three against one—four if you counted the teenager—and that was simply not fair. Alexandra did not expect what happened next.

The tall stranger turned and addressed the three boys, speaking in a low and menacing voice. "You boys bother this kid again and your mamas won't know what happened to your scrawny little butts. Kids like you can get lost real easy in the mountains. If I so much as hear that you or any of your friends ever bother her again, you'll hear from Garret Coulson, personally."

Practically tripping over each other, the three boys hastily fled from the schoolroom, leaving Alexandra alone with Garret. Leaning down on his bent knee, Garret pulled Alexandra toward him and gently brushed away her tears with the back of his hand. He smiled at the trembling child.

"Thank you," she whispered, blinking away tears, her thick dark lashes heavy with dampness.

"My name is Garret. What's yours?" he asked in a gentle voice.

"Alexandra Maria Chamberlain," she said, now smiling.

"Whoa, that's some big name for such a little thing." He chuckled and then gave her mop of dark curls a gentle rustle with one of his hands.

"You saved me. They were gonna kill me."

"I don't think they would actually kill you, Alexandra Maria Chamberlain. But I do believe they were gonna pester you a bit. Don't worry; they won't be bothering you again. And if they do, you just come tell me. I'm in your mama's eleven o'clock class." Garret gave her a wink, his blue eyes twinkling.

Without hesitation, Alexandra threw herself at Garret and wrapped her arms around his neck, holding on tightly. She hugged him. Startled by the gesture, it took Garret a moment to gently release himself from her grip, yet not before she declared, "I love you, Garret. You're my hero."

Holding her at arm's length, Garret studied her face.

"You, Alexandra Maria Chamberlain, are going to be a heartbreaker."

WHEN MRS. CHAMBERLAIN RETURNED TO HER ROOM A FEW moments later, Garret could tell his teacher was surprised to see him, in spite of the fact she had told him to wait in the classroom until she returned from the office. The Chamberlain family was new to Coulson, and it was obvious to Garret this teacher didn't know how things worked in his family's town. Sonny, his older brother, was certainly never reprimanded by a teacher, and he was no angel.

By the expression on Mrs. Chamberlain's face, it was apparent one or more of her colleagues had since filled her in. Earlier that day, when she'd initially demanded Garret return to her class after school, she'd worn a far more confident expression. Unbeknownst to the teacher, her students' chorus of "uh-oh" following her demand was not a warning to Garret that he was about to get in trouble—*but to her*.

Garret wasn't a total delinquent. He never started fights in class, and no one dared provoke him. It wasn't just his name but his size and reputation. Instead of overt belligerence toward his teachers, he treated them dismissively. Blatantly ignoring seating charts, if he wanted to sit next to the prettiest girl in class, he did, often sending the poor guy whose seat he had just commandeered scrambling to find somewhere else to sit. If he wanted to wander into class five minutes late, then his teacher would have to deal with it. Garret Coulson had his own schedule.

"Mommy!" Alexandra raced to her mother and leapt into her arms, giving her a welcoming hug. "Garret is my new friend. He saved my life!"

"Did he now?" Beth eyed Garret curiously. She set Alexandra on her feet. "Alex dear, please go sit very quietly at Mommy's desk. I need to have a private talk with your new friend."

Alex nodded energetically then raced across the room to her mother's desk. En route, she flashed Garret a smile. Beth faced her student.

"Do you want to know what happened?" Garret noticed his teacher appeared more confident than she had moments earlier.

"You mean with my daughter?"

"Yes."

"No, I imagine Alex will tell me all about it on the way home. I'd rather talk about you."

"Me?"

"That's why I asked you to come here today."

"Yeah, well, I came. But I'm gonna get out of here now." Tucking his hands in the back pockets of his denims, he shifted restlessly.

"No, I'd like you to sit down, please." Beth motioned to a chair.

Prepared to ignore the teacher's demand and walk out of the classroom, Garret glanced at Alexandra, who watched him with keen interest. He couldn't bring himself to treat his teacher with disrespect with her young daughter watching. For some reason, that felt wrong.

Shrugging as if he didn't care one way or another, Garret sat down. Beth smiled and took the chair next to him.

"I'm worried about you, Garret." Beth kept her voice low, making it difficult for Alexandra to hear the conversation.

"Worried about me?" It wasn't what Garret expected to hear. Instead, he assumed she would begin with *you must respect my rules—follow the class rules*—or something along those lines.

"Garret, your last test scores were impressive, considering you whipped through them in a matter of minutes and didn't bother to check your answers."

"You think I cheated?" Garret asked angrily. He might find such tests total bullshit, but he was no cheater.

"That thought never crossed my mind."

Beth Chamberlain's talk turned into an impassionate plea, urging Garret to recognize his untapped talents. She insisted he was only hurting himself and that he was better than what he presented to the world, and she wanted to see him succeed not because his last name was Coulson—but because he was a unique, intelligent, and talented young man fully capable of succeeding on his own merit.

He might have tuned her out had something about her passion not sparked a distant memory. In that instant, she reminded him of his grandmother Mary Ellen Coulson.

Garret was not quite five years old when his grandmother died. While his memories of her were fleeting and faint, he could still recall quite vividly the day she had died, for he had been the one to find her.

At first, he thought she was sleeping, curled up on the small sofa in the library. He tried waking her, but when she wouldn't stir, he climbed up with her. He removed the pillow she was clutching and tried to take its place. There wasn't much room on the compact piece of furniture, but the two managed to fit.

Fortunately, his father found them before rigor mortis set in, which would have made it necessary to pry Garret from his dead grandmother's arms. The young child didn't understand immediately; his grandmother was never waking up. Weeks after her funeral he would still ask when she was coming home.

Garret did not believe in dwelling in the past or obsessing over what might be lacking in his life. Because of this, he didn't consider—or remember—it was his grandmother Mary Ellen who had petted and adored him, frequently telling him he was both special and bright. It was a conversation he never had with his own mother, who seemed at times to loathe her middle son.

Garret patiently allowed Beth Chamberlain to have her say, and when she was done, he told her he would consider her words.

———

"So tell me about your new friend," Beth asked her daughter after Garret was gone. Alexandra watched as her mother straightened the classroom so the two could go home.

"Andy Smith and his stupid brother and that stinky Craig Michaels wanted to beat me up. But I ran faster than those stupid boys. And when I got here, Garret told them never to bother me again or he'd make them get lost in the mountains."

Beth turned to face her daughter. "Oh really?" She raised a brow. "You know I don't like you calling people stupid—or stinky for that matter. But what is this about some boys wanting to beat you up? Aren't those boys in your brother's class?"

"Yeah." Alexandra shrugged.

This was the first Beth had heard about bullies from the elementary school next door picking on much younger children.

"Those boys are two years older than you. Why in the world would they pick on a little girl?"

"I'm not some baby," Alexandra protested.

"Why were they chasing you?"

"Well," Alex began, guiltily looking down at her feet, "maybe 'cause I kicked that dummy Andy Smith."

"Oh, Alex, why did you kick Andy?"

"He said he was glad Tommy was sick today and hoped he would never come back."

"That's not a very nice thing for him to have said, but you shouldn't have kicked him. From now on, you need to ignore those older boys when they say mean things. He was just trying to upset you."

"Well, I kicked him good."

CHAPTER TWO

*S*he was probably the hottest thing he had seen since coming to Clement Falls. By the way she was dressed, he doubted she was a local. The woman had class. She reminded him of that broad whose husband was running for president, Kennedy. Of course, this dame was a redhead, but her hair was fixed the same way, and she had a similar look and body type.

"Gina, any idea who that broad is, the redhead?" Anthony nodded toward the dirt parking lot, where the woman stood by a white Cadillac, speaking to several other women.

Wrestling with her squirming toddler, Gina looked to see whom her brother was talking about. Gina tired easily these days. She had begged Anthony to stop a moment after visiting the small market so she could rest.

"Yes, I do. That's Vera Coulson. But you stay away from her, you hear me. You don't want to get in trouble."

"What's so special about her?" Anthony took a drag off his cigarette, still eying the woman.

"Her family are big shots. Her last name is Coulson. *Coulson*, Anthony. She is a very important woman."

"You mean like that town near here?"

"Yes. She's married anyway, so leave her alone."

Gina stood up, the child in her arms. "Come, Anthony, I'm ready to go home now."

"You go. I want to finish my cigarette. Leave the groceries, I'll bring them."

Gina glanced warily from her brother to Vera Coulson. Her little girl started to fuss; it was time for her dinner.

"Okay, Anthony, but please don't do anything." Holding onto the handrail, Gina carried the toddler as she awkwardly made her way down the wooden steps. It would be a short walk to the boardinghouse she owned with her husband.

Anthony Marino leaned back in the Adirondack chair, enjoying the view. It wasn't the quaint, rustic décor of the mountain market or the thick pine forest he found interesting, it was the woman. This might be just what he needed to ease his boredom while things cooled down back home.

He had no intention of following his kid sister's advice. No one told Anthony Marino what to do. The fact the woman was married didn't discourage his interest; it simply upped the ante and made the game more challenging. The redhead laughed at something one of the other women said, and it looked as if they were preparing to get into their vehicles. Disappointed that she was leaving, his hope was renewed when she began walking toward the market as her friends got into their cars to drive away.

VERA GLANCED AT HER WATCH. SHE NEEDED TO GET OFF THE

mountain; it would be getting dark soon, and she hated driving the road from Clement Falls to Coulson at night. She had smoked her last cigarette on the drive up the mountain, but that was hours ago. A quick stop at the market to pick up a pack and she could be on her way.

Attending the Clement Falls Historical Society's lecture had not been her idea. A dreary event, she didn't understand why her husband, Harrison, had urged her to go. It should be enough that Coulson Enterprises had funded the recent restoration of the small mountain museum. Forced to chat and make tedious small talk with the ladies of the historical society, Vera wondered how her life had come to this. She was bored, lonely, and dissatisfied. Now in her early forties, she was beginning to feel old.

Starting up the wood steps of the porch, she noticed a man sitting on one of the two Adirondack chairs adjacent to the market's front entrance. Staring at her, he silently smoked his cigarette. He made no attempt to divert his eyes; instead, they looked her up and down as if inspecting the merchandise.

Vera felt herself blush—and she never blushed. Normally, she would have taken offence at his blatant perusal, but he was so damn handsome, she was flattered. *When was the last time a man looked at me like that—especially such a good-looking man?*

It was impossible to tell how tall he was, since he was sitting down, but he was obviously a large muscular man. Italian, she guessed, with his brown eyes and jet-black hair styled in a rakish pompadour. Dressed in a silk shirt, tailored slacks, and imported leather shoes, he was definitely not from Clement Falls—or Coulson. On closer inspection, she realized he was probably a couple of years older than she was, and she wondered briefly if he colored his hair. *He utterly seethes with sex appeal*, she thought.

Instead of a dismissive glare, which was more her style, Vera flashed Anthony one of her rare smiles and went into the store to get cigarettes. When she came back outside, he was still in the chair.

"Do you mind if I sit down?" she asked impulsively.

"I was hoping you would." He smiled up at her while leaning back in his chair.

She smiled again and sat down.

"I hope you don't mind, but I wanted to have a cigarette before I head off the mountain." After she said it, she realized it was a foolish thing to ask, considering he had been smoking just moments before.

"Please, go ahead," he said.

Vera tore opened the pack she had just purchased and pulled out a cigarette. Anthony had his lighter ready. Flashing a flirtatious smile, she put the cigarette in her mouth and allowed him to light its end. She inhaled deeply and then exhaled.

"Thank you. Are you vacationing up here?" Vera asked, eyeing him with interest.

"What, don't I look like a local?" He chuckled.

"Hardly." She flashed him a smile.

"I'm Anthony Marino." He put out his hand in greeting. Vera was about to shift her cigarette from her right hand to her left so she could accept the friendly gesture, when he abruptly took hold of her left hand. He held it for a moment and looked at her wedding ring.

"I was hoping there wasn't a ring," he said with a boyish pout. "Perhaps you are a widow? A man might hope."

She laughed and withdrew her hand. "Shame on you for sounding so cheerful at the possibility."

"A man can dream."

"My name is Vera Coulson. The last time I checked, my husband was quite alive. But you didn't answer my question."

"I'm visiting my sister and her husband. They have a boardinghouse up here."

"Staying long?" she asked, her blue-grey eyes sparkling.

"Only if you give me a reason," he whispered.

"Oh, Mr. Marino, you do know how to flatter an old married woman."

"Old? Hardly. I might accuse you of fishing for compliments, but considering how you look, I imagine you get them all the time."

Vera found herself blushing again. It had been years since she had exchanged such flirty banter with an attractive man.

"Well, thank you, kind sir." *I may have dreaded the ride up to Clement Falls today, but at least I'll go home with a smile on my face.* "I hope you enjoy your visit."

"Actually," Anthony began as he took out a cigarette and lit it, "I've been considering finding a place to stay in Coulson. Weather's turning and I'd rather not be here when the snow starts falling next month."

"So this isn't just a short visit?"

"I have no immediate plans. You might say I'm in limbo while working on a couple of business deals. Came up here to see my kid sister; I practically raised her myself. So I like to check on her from time to time. Make sure my brother-in-law is doing her right."

"While Coulson is a small town, it's much larger than Clement Falls. I imagine you'll find more to occupy your time there than up here."

"Can I be candid with you, Mrs. Coulson?"

17

"Only if you call me Vera." She flashed him another smile.

"I probably won't be around this area for more than six months. I know you're married and maybe happily married. I have no idea. But if you ever want some company—something to break up the monotony, I want you to know I would be interested. Your husband would never have to find out."

"Mr. Marino, are you suggesting what I think you are? I just met you two minutes ago."

"Life is short, pretty lady. As we get older, we realize opportunities don't come along that often, and if we don't try grabbing what we want, we'll never get anything. And frankly I want you."

Vera stared at Anthony in stunned silence. While she knew he was flirting with her, she had never expected such a blatant proposal.

"Have I shocked you? I apologize if I offended you. But I had to say it. I've never met a woman who I felt such an immediate attraction to. Don't you feel it at all? Am I imagining it?"

There was something so sweet and heartfelt in his inquiry that she found it impossible to guard her feelings. "Well," she said shyly, "I confess I find you very attractive. But, like I said, I'm a married woman."

"I respect your feelings. I've been married. Had my wives been more like you, I would probably still be married."

"Why do you say that?" Vera asked.

"When I was really young, my wife died in childbirth."

"I'm sorry."

"It was rough. Took me a few years to get married again. But just a few months into the marriage, I found her cheating with one of my friends. I suppose I should have realized marriage was not for me, but I gave it another try."

"What happened?"

"She decided marriage wasn't for her, so she just took off. Technically speaking, I guess I'm still married. But I haven't seen her for a few years." Smashing his cigarette butt on the patio, he placed his hand over hers and gave it a gentle squeeze. "Do you ever ask yourself why it is so wrong to give in to your deepest desires? Especially when there is no reason for anyone to ever find out. It doesn't have to change your life, but for a few hours...what I would give to have just a few hours with you."

He lifted her hand to his mouth and kissed the back of it before releasing it. "I'm sorry. I know this is totally inappropriate of me. Please forgive me." He sounded sincerely contrite.

"No...I mean...well, I confess I'm flattered."

"I hope your husband takes good care of you," he told her. "If you were my woman, well, I sure as hell wouldn't let you come up here by yourself. My woman wouldn't be running around alone, especially if she looked like you."

"Are you one of those old-fashioned men who expect their women to do as they are told?" She flashed him an impish smile, then noticed his expression was more serious than she expected. She found it unsettling and yet in some way titillating.

Reaching out with one hand, he captured her chin and tilted her face so he could look into her eyes. "If you were my woman and I found you alone, talking to a man like myself, I would drag you home and remind you who you belonged to. It would be a lesson you would never forget," he said in a whisper.

Wide eyed, Vera was speechless. His passion both frightened and excited her. If Harrison stumbled upon her flirting with the stranger, he would be nothing more than mildly amused. When she had told her husband he was no longer welcome in her bed, he had accepted her decree with as much outrage as if she had announced a change in linen colors. She imagined Anthony Marino would not timidly accept such a decree but would take what he wanted. Her heart raced at the thought.

Anthony leaned closer and brushed a kiss across her lips before pulling away. He stood up.

"Go home, pretty lady. Before I forget myself and take you to some nice little cabin where I can show you just what I expect from my woman."

Still speechless, Vera sat alone on the porch as she watched the dark stranger walk away carrying a sack of groceries.

CHAPTER THREE

*L*ocals called it *Coulson House*, an understated characterization of the property. Located on a hill-top, it seemed oddly out of place in its high-desert southwest location. Its classic architecture bespoke a building better suited for a city that had witnessed a significant passage of time instead of one that had barely been in existence for a decade.

Well-manicured palm trees majestically lined the long winding concrete drive from the street below to the massive estate situated on a five-acre parcel. Pinyon pine trees dotted the perimeter of the property. Within a year after the structure was built, Randall Coulson had a lawn planted, transforming the barren dirt surrounding Coulson House into a lush green carpet.

As a small child, Garret and his older brother, Harrison Junior, or Sonny as his family called him, played hide-and-seek on the rarely used third floor of the mansion. Garret learned to be quick-witted when playing such games with his brother, or else he would find himself locked in some trunk or cupboard for an indefinite length of time.

Parking his truck in the front drive, Garret noticed his brother's green MGB sports car. *Sonny is home*, he thought. Getting quickly from his vehicle, he slammed the door shut before racing to the front entrance. He found his grandfather, father, and older brother all in the living room, enjoying evening cocktails. Sonny shared the leather couch with their father, Harrison. Garret's grandfather Randall sat on the large leather recliner facing the two men.

"When did you get home?" Garret asked after he sprinted into the room and plopped down on an empty chair.

"About thirty minutes ago," Sonny told him as he took a sip of his drink. Over six years separated Sonny and Garret. The brothers weren't close, but it wasn't the age difference; Garret simply disliked his older sibling. Yet there was no doubt they were brothers. Both bore a striking resemblance to their father, Harrison.

People said Harrison Senior inherited his blue eyes from his mother, Mary Ellen. Harrison's father, Randall, had dark brown eyes, and while he was a tall man, he wasn't as tall as his son. Now in his early seventies, Randall continued to be active and as fit as any man twenty years his junior.

"Don't you have classes?" Garret asked.

"Your brother has decided he's finished with college," Harrison explained. He sounded slightly annoyed.

"Dad, I've got my bachelor's. You and Grandfather didn't even finish college."

"That was different," Harrison insisted.

"Oh, leave the boy alone," Randall said. "He's right, you know. We did fine without finishing college. And he's a Coulson. We make our own rules."

"Well, I do have my degree." Sonny sounded insulted. "I

just realized there was no reason to get my master's. Waste of time."

Garret sat quietly and watched as the three men debated Sonny's future with the family business. *I do have my degree*, his brother had insisted. Garret then recalled a conversation he had overheard between his brother and another college student. Sonny had been paying someone to take his tests—write his term papers. Garret wondered if his father or grandfather knew or cared.

Remembering that afternoon's conversation with his algebra teacher, Mrs. Chamberlain, Garret asked himself, *Do I want to be like my older brother?* He didn't doubt Sonny would have a financially stable future. His brother had the support of their wealthy grandfather. But the thought of living his entire life dependent on the controlling man, never accomplishing anything on his own merit, troubled Garret. He wasn't sure if it was Mrs. Chamberlain's private lecture or listening to his grandfather and father plan his older brother's life, but in that moment, Garret Coulson knew he had less than two years of high school to turn his academic future around.

"Does this mean you're staying here?" Garret asked, breaking into the conversation. He had been so lost in his own private thoughts he hadn't really heard what they had been saying.

"I guess you weren't listening." Garret's father sounded annoyed.

"Grandfather feels it would be good for me to see more of the world before I start work." Wherever he was going, Sonny seemed pleased. "I'll be traveling abroad."

"How does Mother feel about this? Where is she, anyway?" Garret asked.

"She should be home soon," Harrison said. "She was at

that lecture up at Clement Falls this afternoon." Harrison glanced at his watch. "Although I'm a little surprised she isn't home yet."

"So you actually convinced her to go?" Garret asked.

"Someone from the family needed to be there, and your father and I had meetings all afternoon," Randall said.

"Does she know Sonny is home?" Garret asked.

His question would be answered in the next minute when Vera Coulson sailed through the front door.

"Is that Sonny's car?" she asked, hurrying into the room. When she saw her eldest son, she rushed to him and gave him a hug.

When Sonny started to explain the reason for his unexpected arrival, Vera interrupted him and said, "You can tell me all about it, dear, over dinner. Let me run upstairs and freshen up." She dashed from the room as quickly as she had arrived.

The four men chatted for a few minutes longer when Garret's younger brother, Russell, ran into the living room to announce dinner was about to be served. Everyone stood up, agreeing the conversation could be resumed in the dining room.

Harrison and Randall lingered in the living room for a few minutes, discussing business, while the three brothers walked toward the dining room. Neither man noticed when Sonny shoved his foot in Russell's path, causing the eight-year-old boy to trip and fall to the floor.

"Why did you do that?" Garret asked angrily. He leaned down and pulled his younger brother to his feet. Russell glared at Sonny, refusing to cry.

"Because it's fun," Sonny said with a laugh. He was still laughing when he walked into the dining room and was greeted by his mother, who gave him a second welcome hug.

Shaking his head in disgust, Garret patted Russell's shoulder and gave the boy a quick wink. There were times Garret found the kid annoying, but he figured that was simply the nature of little brothers. He didn't see any reason to go out of his way to make the kid's life miserable.

Thrilled to have her favorite son home, Vera clutched Sonny's left arm as he walked her to the right side of the table, where the two took seats next to each other. Garret and Russell sat on the opposite side while Harrison and Randall took their places at opposing ends of the table.

"So tell me, Sonny, to what do we owe the honor of your visit?" Vera asked.

"I've decided not to get my master's."

"You've dropped out of school?" She looked over at him.

"It's only been a month, no big deal." Sonny shrugged.

"Says the boy who is not paying for his own tuition," Randall grumbled.

"I thought you were okay with this, Grandfather?" Sonny asked.

"You miss the point. If you recall, I thought getting a master's in the first place was a waste of money. You have all the degree you need. Would have saved me some money had you just listened."

"So what are your plans? Are you staying here, working for your grandfather?" Vera sounded hopeful.

"Grandfather says it will do me good to have a European tour before starting work."

"You're traveling abroad?" Vera looked from her son to her husband. "It would be nice if you took me to Europe."

"This is my father's idea," Harrison told her. "But if you wish to do some traveling, no one's stopping you."

"Alone? Or perhaps I could go with Sonny," Vera suggested.

Garret glanced at his older brother and chuckled. Sonny's expression was priceless, and Garret almost felt sorry for him, yet not quite. *It would serve the idiot right if Mother tagged along on his big European adventure.*

"I don't think so," Randall chimed in. The tension in Sonny's face drained, replaced with a look of relief. "A young man does not take a trip such as this with his mother."

"I suppose not," Vera reluctantly agreed.

The table was silent for a few minutes while they ate.

"I thought John was joining us for dinner this evening?" Vera asked.

"No, John had to fly off at the last minute this afternoon, putting out fires," Randall explained as he helped himself to a roll.

"John Weber?" Sonny asked. "Is he still doing your dirty work, Grandfather?"

"He does not do my *dirty work*, Sonny. John Weber is a very effective troubleshooter for Coulson Enterprises. And if you intend to take part in the family business, I expect you to speak more respectfully toward valuable members of the company," Randall snapped.

"I was just kidding, Grandfather."

"Sometimes your humor escapes me," Randall said.

"It's because he isn't funny," Garret said under his breath between bites. From across the table Sonny gave him a swift kick. Garret silently glared at his older brother.

"So how was the lecture?" Harrison asked his wife.

"Boring, how did you expect it to be?" she asked.

"Well, did you enjoy it at all? It's usually lovely up in Clement Falls this time of year."

"I suppose. A very handsome man flirted with me."

"Someone from the museum looking for a donation?" Harrison asked.

"No." Vera glared at Harrison. "He was just some man I met when I stopped at the market."

"Well, that explains why you were so late," Harrison said, yet he didn't seem upset.

"Mother, picking up men at Clement Falls now?" Garret teased.

"Hardly." Vera glared at her middle son.

"Did he know who you were?" Randall asked.

"Why do you ask that?" Vera frowned at her father-in-law.

"You need to be careful, Vera. All sorts of unscrupulous men out there waiting to take advantage of someone in your position."

"What do you mean in my position?"

"I'm sure you know exactly what I mean."

"I find that insulting, Randall. Basically you're saying the only reason a man might flirt with me is because I'm married to your son?"

"I didn't realize having strange men flirt with you was so important," Randall said.

"Good lord, I never said it was important. I simply made a comment that a man flirted with me, and the only conclusion you can arrive at is that someone wants something from *you*."

Randall started to comment, but Harrison interrupted, saying, "Dad, I'm constantly amazed at how little you know about women." He turned to look at Vera. "I apologize for my teasing. I didn't mean to start—this. You are a very attractive woman, and I see no reason why a man wouldn't flirt with you." Harrison paused for a moment then asked, "Russell, hand me the rolls, please."

"I need someone to drive me to Tommy Chamberlain's

house tonight," Russell said as he handed his father the basket of rolls.

"Who is Tommy Chamberlain?" Vera took a sip of her wine.

"He's a boy in my class. His family moved here this summer."

"Why do you need to go there on a school night?" Vera asked him.

"Tommy was sick today, so the teacher asked if someone would take him his schoolwork. I volunteered."

"That was generous of you." Vera sounded annoyed.

"My driver can take you," Randall told Russell. "You do know where this boy lives?"

"Thanks, Grandfather. Yeah, I know. Ryan Keller told me."

"Who's Ryan Keller?" Randall asked. He couldn't recall a Keller family.

"He's also new this year."

"There are a lot of new people moving into Coulson," Randall said with a smile, pleased the city he'd founded— that bore his name—was growing.

CHAPTER FOUR

"*B*eth, a limousine just pulled up in the driveway." George Chamberlain held the lace curtain to one side as he looked out his living room window. "And I'll be damned, that looks like a chauffeur driving the car."

"In Coulson?" Beth walked from the kitchen while drying her hands on a dishtowel. She had just finished washing up the dinner dishes. Beth peeked out the window and watched as the chauffeur opened the back door of the vehicle and let out a small boy. He appeared to be about the same age as their son, Tommy. The chauffeur stayed by the car as the child ran up to their front door. He carried a stack of papers.

Beth opened the door before the boy had time to ring the doorbell.

"Hello." Beth greeted him with a smile.

"Hello, I'm Russell Coulson. I'm in Tommy's class. I brought him his schoolwork."

Coulson, well, that explains the limousine and chauffeur, Beth thought. She guessed he was Garret's younger brother.

There was a strong family resemblance; they both had remarkable blue eyes. But the younger Coulson had blond hair while his brother's hair was dark.

Russell started to hand her the papers, but when she reached for them, he abruptly pulled them back.

"Can I see Tommy?" he asked.

Beth smiled and moved to one side so he could come in the house. She glanced outside to the driveway and noticed the chauffeur didn't appear to be in a hurry to go anywhere.

"Should we invite your driver in?" Beth asked before shutting the door.

"Nah, he'd rather wait by the car. He told me so."

"Okay." Beth shrugged and shut the door. In the living room, George had moved to the couch and had turned on the television. Beth led Russell to the hallway leading to Tommy's bedroom.

Walking down the hallway, Russell heard girls' voices coming from a room ahead. The door was open. As he and Beth passed the room's doorway, he glanced in and saw two little girls sitting on the floor, playing dolls. The girls stopped what they were doing and looked up at him but said nothing. As he continued down the hallway, the smaller of the two girls dropped her doll and ran to the doorway to see who was with her mother. Russell didn't look back, so he didn't know Tommy's youngest sister was staring at him.

"Tommy, you have a visitor," Beth said as she opened the door to her son's bedroom.

Wearing pajamas, Tommy sat on his bed, sorting through his baseball cards. He looked up to see who it was.

"Hi," Russell greeted him as he glanced around the bedroom.

"Hi, Russell, what're you doing here?" Tommy tossed his cards in a heap on the center of the bed then moved so that he was sitting along the edge of the mattress, his bare feet dangling to the floor.

"Russell, you can go on in. According to the doctor, Tommy isn't contagious anymore. Tommy, Russell brought your schoolwork."

"Oh, drat," Tommy said as Russell handed him the stack of papers.

"I'll leave you boys to chat a bit." Beth left the room.

"There really isn't much," Russell assured him. "Just some stupid stuff, you can do it pretty fast."

Tommy glanced briefly at the papers and then tossed them on the floor. Russell sat on the mattress with Tommy. The two boys started looking through the baseball cards as they talked.

"So nothing happened at school today?" Tommy asked.

"Nuthin' much."

"My sister Alex kicked Andy Smith in the ankle after school."

"He's a badass. Did he sock her?"

"Nah, she can run pretty fast for a girl. But she needs to stop doing stupid stuff like that. She's gonna get pounded."

"Yep, Andy Smith has no problem pounding girls."

"He ever bother you?"

"Nah, no one ever bugs me."

"You ever hit girls?" Tommy wanted to smack his sisters sometimes, but his father wouldn't let him.

"Nope. Garret would pound me if I hit a girl."

"Garret?"

"He's my brother. Goes to the high school."

"It's pretty weird to have the high school next door. Where we used to live, it was across town."

"Last year it was all one school. You have any brothers?"

"No, just two apey sisters. You have any sisters?"

"No. Just two brothers."

"That's cool. I wish I had a brother instead of apey sisters."

"Sometimes brothers can be pretty apey too."

BETH STOOD AT HER FRONT DOOR AND WATCHED AS RUSSELL Coulson raced to the limousine parked in her driveway. A few minutes later, after the car pulled away, she closed the door then joined her husband in the living room.

"I believe that's the brother of the boy I was telling you about earlier." Beth sat next to George. Pulling her bare feet onto the sofa, she leaned against her husband.

"I heard him say his name was Coulson." He put his arm around his wife's shoulder and gave her a little pat.

"From what I understand, there are three sons. The oldest is in college, the middle son is in my class, and the one that just raced out the door, that's the youngest."

"The one in your class, the one Alex raved about at the dinner table, that's your troublemaker?"

"I wouldn't say troublemaker exactly, just too cool to follow the rules. But after today, I learned something about that boy."

Unbeknownst to Beth and George, their eldest daughter was standing in the hallway eavesdropping on their conversation.

"What's that?"

"I always knew that boy wasn't all spit and fire. He has a little softness, and I'm hoping to find where he's hidden his brains."

"I imagine it's where most sixteen-year-old boys have their brains." They both laughed. Alex raced back to her bedroom before her little sister, Katie, tattled on her. They weren't supposed to eavesdrop on their parents; her mother said it was rude. But she wondered what her parents found so funny.

"Did that boy go home?" Katie asked Alexandra when she returned to the bedroom. A year younger than her sister, Katie looked like an Alexandra miniature.

"I didn't see him in the living room, so I guess so." Alexandra sat back on the floor with her sister and began putting clothes on her doll.

"Were you scared when those boys chased you?" Katie asked.

"No. They were just dopy boys. They didn't scare me." Alex sounded as if she meant it.

"Do you like it here?" Katie looked at her sister.

"You mean our new house?"

"Yeah. I miss Grandma." Katie sounded sad.

"Me too. But Mom says she's coming to spend Christmas with us," Alex reminded her.

"That's a long time from now."

"I know. Do you like kindergarten?"

"Yeah, it's fun. Do you like first grade?" Katie asked.

"Not as fun as kindergarten."

"Alex, please don't kick those big boys again. I don't want you to get socked."

"Don't worry, Katie. I can run real fast." *Plus I have a protector*.

"What are you two doing?" Tommy asked from the doorway.

"Playing dolls. Want to play?" Katie asked.

"No way." Tommy made a stink face.

Katie shrugged and went back to playing with her doll.

"Who was that boy?" Alex asked.

Tommy walked into the room and sat on one of the two twin beds. "Russell. He's in my class. He brought over my schoolwork."

"Mom says you're going back to school on Monday."

"Yeah, I can't wait!"

"You don't like staying home with Dad?" Katie sounded surprised.

"It's okay. But there's nothing to do here."

"You could always play dolls with us," Katie said.

Tommy rolled his eyes, jumped off the bed, and kicked at the doll clothes, scattering them over the floor, before heading back to his room.

"Boys are stupid," Katie whispered when Tommy left the room.

"I know," Alex agreed.

HARRISON AND RANDALL SAT IN THE LIBRARY AT COULSON House, smoking cigars, when Russell returned from the Chamberlains' house.

The eight-year-old poked his head in the room for a brief moment. "Thanks, Grandfather!" He didn't wait for a response but dashed down the hall and up the staircase to his bedroom. Randall chuckled.

"That boy is always on the go. Reminds me of you when you were his age."

"I don't know about that, but he's a sharp one and he doesn't seem to get in trouble like his older brothers."

"Boys are supposed to shake things up at their age," Randall said.

"I suppose." Harrison flicked an ash into a pottery bowl

on the table next to his chair. "You know, Mother would skin us if she caught us smoking in her library."

"Yes, she would. Sometimes I wonder if she's here, watching us." Randall glanced to the sofa where they had found her body.

"Dad, don't you ever think of getting married again?"

"Lord, at my age, whatever for?"

"I don't know. Companionship—*love*."

"Harrison, your mother was the only woman for me. I'm quite content with my life."

They were silent for a moment before Harrison broached another topic.

"Dad, do you think it's a good idea for Sonny to take this Europe trip alone? He's awful young."

"Nonsense, you were married and had a child by the time you were his age. And you'd traveled to Europe."

"Yes, when I was in the service—during the war. I hate to say it, but that boy is awful immature, in spite of the fact he's graduated from college."

"Then this trip will do him some good. Let him experience a broader view of the world."

Upstairs, Garret was in Sonny's room, watching his brother unpack his suitcases.

"So why unpack?" Casually sprawled across his brother's bed, Garret picked up a cigarette off Sonny's nightstand and lit it.

"What kind of question is that?" Sonny glanced at his brother. "Get your damn shoes off my bed."

"Don't get all bent." Garret shrugged and sat up, setting his feet on the floor. Flicking ashes on the carpet, he took another drag off the cigarette. "This is shitty weed. When did you start smoking menthol? You a girl or something?" Garret smashed the lit cigarette in the ashtray, putting it out.

"Go buy your own fucking smokes." Sonny tossed his empty suitcases in the closet.

"I thought the old man was sending you on some trip. Figured you'd be packing instead of unpacking," Garret said.

"You jealous?"

"Not especially."

"I hear those French girls are really hot." Sonny sat on the edge of his desk and looked over at his younger brother. "Figured I'd fuck my way through Europe."

"Because you can't get any here?"

"I get plenty. Just looking forward to something different."

Bored with the conversation, Garret stood up.

"That explains what happened to your brain," Garret said as he walked to the door.

"What's that supposed to mean?" Sonny scowled.

"You fucked your brain out." Garret laughed as he walked from the room. A moment later Sonny slammed his door shut. Walking down the hall, still chuckling, Garret noticed his younger brother, Russell, was looking out his doorway.

"Hey, squirt." Garret smiled at Russell.

"Is he really leaving again?" Russell whispered. Stepping out into the hallway, the young boy glanced over at his eldest brother's closed door.

"That's what they say. Haven't heard when. Can't be soon enough, as far as I'm concerned."

"Garret, why is Sonny the way he is?"

"You mean an asshole?"

"You aren't supposed to use words like that."

Garret laughed and then tousled his brother's blond hair. "You gonna rat me out, kid?"

"No." Russell looked somewhat offended that Garret would suggest such a thing. Russell could not recall a time Sonny actually lived at Coulson House. He was always off at college, but he did visit on occasional weekends and holidays. They weren't visits Russell looked forward to, as Sonny enjoyed tormenting him.

"Sonny—is Sonny. But lucky for us the schmuck won't be here for long," Garret cheerfully reminded him.

CHAPTER FIVE

"*A*nthony, I don't think this is a good idea," Gina told her brother. She watched as he packed his suitcase. Fifteen minutes earlier, he had tossed it on the bed after announcing he was leaving the boardinghouse.

"There's nothing for me to do up here. I'm about to go crazy from boredom." He continued to pack.

"It's that woman, isn't it?" Gina asked.

"What woman?"

"The Coulson woman, I saw how you looked at her. Please don't try starting anything with her. I thought you came up here to lie low for a while until things settle down in Long Island. You don't want to draw attention to yourself."

"You worry too much, Gina. I can take care of myself." He closed his suitcase and lifted it off the bed. After kissing his sister's cheek, he headed out the door.

Gina stood on her front porch and watched as Anthony got into his car and drove off.

"Is he gone?" Nick asked, walking into the living room. Gina continued to stand at the open door.

"Why didn't you make him stay?" Gina asked.

"Your brother has never listened to me. And frankly, I'm glad he's gone." Nick walked over to the door and closed it. Gina turned and looked at her husband.

"He's my brother," she said, tears in her eyes.

"And if he wasn't your brother, I never would have put up with him for as long as I have. I don't like him around my family. He makes me nervous. Your brother is a dangerous man, you know that."

"He loves me," Gina whispered, tears swimming in her large brown eyes. Nick pulled her into his arms and held her.

"I love you too, Gina. I want you safe." He kissed the top of her head.

Cliffwood Motel was built the same year as Coulson House. Unlike the stately mansion, whose primary function was to impress potential property owners and show the world Randall Coulson was committed to the ambitious development project, speed and price dictated the motel's construction. Time had not been kind to the inferior structure, which looked twice its actual age.

For Wally Keller, Cliffwood Motel's dilapidated state made it possible for him to afford the purchase of the run-down commercial property. Had the motel been located in an isolated area or on the outskirts of town, it would not have suited his needs. After all, he had two sons to consider. Two sons he was raising on his own.

He had worked in construction since he was a teenager, so when renovating the motel, he could do most of the labor himself. Becoming a business owner had never been his dream, but after his wife's death two years earlier, he found it increasingly difficult to be both a mother and father to his boys while working outside the home in his construction job.

It was his sister who had showed him the ad for the motel. He had never been to the Coulson area, but she had and she believed it would be perfect for her brother and nephews. He had a little inheritance money from his parents' estate, which had enabled him to purchase the motel. It would serve as both income property and home for his family.

Located on the end of Main Street in the original section of downtown Coulson, the motel was within walking distance to most of the shops, stores, and restaurants in that section of town.

Since moving to Coulson during the summer, he had worked primarily on the living quarters he shared with his sons. It included a small living room, kitchen, two large bedrooms, one bathroom, and a connecting office where hotel guests could register. A long counter separated the living quarters from the office, enabling him to be with his sons at night while taking care of guests if necessary.

He intended to start renovating the hotel rooms—all twenty of them—by November. Over the summer, he had managed to rent the rooms to vacationing fishermen and hunters, who weren't put off by the primitive quarters. He was still getting fishermen on the weekends, but it was typically dead during the week.

Wally Keller was surprised when the well-dressed man walked into his office, asking to rent a room for an indefinite amount of time. "How long did you say you want a room for?" Wally wondered if he had heard the man correctly.

"A month, maybe longer."

Wally eyed the stranger. He could use the business, but the man didn't look like one of his typical guests. When the stranger had first walked in the office door, Wally thought he was going to ask for directions. He looked like a man dressed for a night on the town—just not this town.

"So what brings you to Coulson?" Wally asked as he opened the reservation book.

"I'm checking into a couple of business opportunities in the area. I've been staying with my sister up at Clement Falls, and it's starting to get cold up there. I'm not a fan of the snow."

"I understand it can snow up in Clement Falls in November. But they say our winters in Coulson are mild. Even sunny. Hope that's true."

"So you're new in town?"

"I just bought this place—this past June. It's my first season. But I'll warn you, the rooms are a little primitive. I would love your business, but I'm not sure you'll be happy here. Would you like to check out the room before you register?"

"No, that's fine. Your rates look reasonable, and I might be around here for a while before I get things settled. No reason to spend a fortune when I don't intend to spend much time in the room. I'd like the one on the end—room ten—if it's free."

"Sure. Can I have your name, please."

"Marino. Anthony Marino."

THE FIRST THING ANTONY DID WHEN HE ENTERED THE SMALL motel room was to open the window and let in the fresh air. He doubted the room had been rented for a while, because it smelled musty. He wasn't surprised to find it clean, despite its need for a facelift. The guy at the liquor store told him Cliffwood Motel was run-down but clean.

He chose this room because of its location to the street and the private walkway that led to its door. One could inconspicuously gain access to the walkway by ducking through the trees behind the public restrooms on Main Street. When the time came for Vera Coulson to meet him at the motel, she could park her car by any of the shops on Main Street and simply walk to the restrooms—and disappear.

Anthony noticed the intriguing access the previous week when taking his sister shopping in the center of town. He went to use the restroom and while coming out of the building heard what sounded like children playing. He wondered briefly if there was some school in the area. Stepping closer to the trees behind the restrooms, he pushed the limbs to one side to have a look. It appeared to be the back of a motel. A long concrete walkway ran along the building. On the far end of the walkway, two boys were tossing a football back and forth. They were the apparent source of the noise. The door closest to him wore a faded number 10. When driving down Main Street later that afternoon, he noticed the street curved to the left. Instead of going north, he was now going west. Cliffwood Motel faced this section of Main Street.

Already thinking of getting out of Clement Falls, he had asked the guy at a liquor store he frequented about the motel. It wasn't until his encounter with Vera did he give the motel another thought.

Tossing his keys on the dresser, he flopped down on the bed and looked up at the ceiling. His hands, their fingers laced together, pillowed the back of his head. Without sitting up, he kicked off his shoes and shoved them off the bed using one foot. They fell with loud thuds to the wood floor.

If things worked out as planned, he should be able to get out of Coulson before spring. Perhaps going back to Long Island wasn't a good idea but maybe LA or Chicago. Until last night, the thought of being stuck in the area for even another week seemed intolerable, yet now he had a new diversion to keep him interested.

He had checked around. The Coulsons had money all right. It seemed they were fairly clean, but the old man might have done some business with the moonshiners back during prohibition. But hell, who hadn't? Kennedy was running for president and his old man was nothing but a moonshiner himself. Of course, running for office wasn't the same as actually getting elected. He didn't care what his sister, Gina, thought; there was no way some Irish-Catholic boy had a chance to get into the White House.

From what he had learned, old man Coulson and his son thought they were some big shots in this little shit resort town. Big fish, little pond, he thought. Men like that imagined they had power, but Anthony knew they were too afraid to grasp real power. Vera Coulson was the reigning princess. It would be fun to fuck the princess of Coulson.

It was obvious to him she wasn't getting what she needed at home. She hadn't even put up a fuss when he had kissed her. Remembering the priceless expression on her face stroked his ego. He was fairly confident she was still thinking of him—maybe even fantasizing about him. It gave him a heady rush of power. Smiling, he moved his hands from behind his head and unbuttoned his slacks. Shifting on the bed to get comfortable and to loosen the fit of his pants, he pulled the zipper down. Shoving his right hand down the front of his slacks, he took hold of his already growing erection.

He would seduce her first—make her feel special. Women liked that, especially when their men were ignoring them. He wouldn't be surprised if her husband had something on the side. Hell, he would be surprised if he didn't.

After he reeled her in, Anthony wanted her lust, not her love. He also wanted her fear. *Lust and fear, not love and fear,* he thought. A woman in love was unpredictable, the love was her driving force, and that held no interest for him. But lust and fear, those were two powerful driving forces he could manipulate. When he was finished with Vera Coulson, she would be the addict and he the heroin.

CHAPTER SIX

*S*itting on a small patch of grass, Alexandra leaned against a tree while enjoying the shade it provided. Chaotic playground sounds—laughter, shouts, childish voices, and an occasional teacher's whistle—seemed more distant than they actually were. Absently tugging individual blades of grass from the dirt, it didn't occur to her that she was damaging the lawn. Instead, she was too busy thinking about Halloween costumes.

Katie wanted to be a princess, but Alexandra wanted to be a gypsy. If she were a gypsy, her mom would have to get her a tambourine. Alex liked the jingly sound of a tambourine. But Mom always wanted the sisters to have matching costumes. Alex didn't think it was fair. Tommy always got to be what he wanted. This year he was going to be a pirate. She knew it was just because he wanted to swing a sword around. Boys were dopy.

"You're gonna get in trouble." A boy's voice broke her concentration. Alex looked up. Jimmy Keller stood over her. Wearing a wrinkled, button-down, green plaid shirt and jeans, he was one of the chubbier first graders. Not quite as tall as Alexandra, he had brownish-red hair and a spattering of freckles across his friendly face. Some of the other kids teased him about his weight, but Alex didn't. She stopped tugging at the blades of grass and frowned.

"Why?" Alex wore one of the new school dresses her mother had purchased at the end of summer. Red and green plaid, with a white Peter Pan collar, it was one of her favorites. The dark fabric concealed any grass stains she might get from sitting on the lawn. Unfortunately, her white socks did not fare as well nor did her new pair of shoes, which were covered with scuff marks due to her habit of rubbing them together while she sat on the ground.

"You're pulling up the grass. Teachers don't like that." Jimmy sat down next to her and looked toward the dodge ball circle, where a spirited game was taking place. One of the players was Jimmy's older brother, Ryan. Another was Russell Coulson, but Alexandra didn't know either boy. Unlike her little sister, Katie, she hadn't gotten a good look at Russell when he had visited her house.

"Why aren't you playing?" Alex asked, nodding to the game of dodge ball taking place.

Jimmy shrugged then asked Alex the same question.

"Maybe if I was a boy."

"But girls are playing." Jimmy watched the game as they talked.

"If I was a boy, I could wear Levi's instead of a dress. Then I'd play." Girls had to wear dresses to school and Alex didn't like the stinging slap of the dodge ball as it hit her bare legs.

"Oh," Jimmy said, not really understanding what she meant.

"What are you going to be for Halloween?" she asked.

"A cowboy. Do they have a very good Halloween here?"

"I don't know. Don't you know?"

"We just moved here over the summer," Jimmy told her.

"Us too. Do you like it?"

"It's okay. We get to see our dad more, which is cool," Jimmy said.

"What about your mom? My mom works next door at the high school."

"My mom died when I was little."

Alex turned her head, looking from the dodge ball game to Jimmy. She had never known anyone who didn't have a mother.

"You don't have a mom?" Alex couldn't believe it.

"No. Not anymore."

"Do you miss her?" Alex asked.

"I guess. It's hard for me to remember sometimes. But Ryan tells me about her."

"Who's Ryan?"

"My older brother. See, that's him playing dodge ball. The one in the red shirt."

Alex looked and wrinkled her nose. The boy appeared to be about her brother's size. She thought her older brother was dopy. Of course, that didn't mean she wouldn't sock a person who said something mean about him.

"So why do you get to see your dad more now?" Alex was fascinated with this boy who had no mother.

"We bought a motel in town. We get to live there. But we have to fix it up. He lets Ryan and me help on weekends. It's my job to pick up all the nails."

"Pick them up from where?"

"From the floor. Lots of nails on the floor when you're building stuff. Doesn't your dad build stuff?"

"No. My dad works with numbers."

"Numbers?" Jimmy scrunched up his nose.

"He's a count-aunt."

"What's that?"

Alex shrugged. "I don't know. He works at the kitchen table with lots of papers. We're not allowed to touch them. Katie spilled a glass of milk on them and got in big trouble last week."

"Katie?"

"My sister. She's just a little kid, in kindergarten."

"You have any brothers?"

"Yeah, a dopy brother in the third grade. He thinks he's so much smarter than me. But he's not."

"My brother's in the third grade too. But he's really smart. Sometimes he lets me hang out with him."

Alex wrinkled her nose in disgust. "I don't like Tommy touching my toys. Once he cut my favorite doll's hair."

Jimmy laughed. Alex scowled at him and then gave him a good punch in the arm.

"Oww!" Jimmy grabbed his injured limb and gave it a rub.

The recess bell rang. Jimmy and Alex jumped up and raced toward the classrooms with the rest of the students on the playground.

Standing on Main Street's sidewalk, scrutinizing the window display, Vera longed for civilization. Harrison insisted she buy her clothes locally—*support the local merchants*, he said. The dresses in Mabel's weren't exactly horrid, but they were last year's fashions. Of course, she doubted if anyone in Coulson would notice.

"That black one was made for you." A male's voice interrupted her thoughts. Vera turned abruptly to the sound of

48

the voice. It was *him*, the man who had kissed her at Clement Falls.

"*You*," she said, unable to mask her surprise.

"Guilty," he said with a chuckle, then stepped closer. Standing next to her, he looked in the store window, his attention focused on the little black dress hanging on a mannequin. "I'd love to see you in it."

"What are you doing here?" She turned to look in the window, not wanting to draw attention to the fact she was standing on Main Street, talking to a strange man.

"After meeting you, I decided to get off that damn mountain and rent a room in town."

"After meeting me? What do I have to do with it?" She glanced askance at Anthony Marino, then quickly moved her gaze back to the window display.

"There was nothing in Clement Falls that caught my interest. And then I met you." He continued to look in the store window.

"You don't even know me, Mr. Marino."

"I know I'd like to get to know you better. I'm glad you remembered my name. But please, call me Anthony. I hope you also remember our kiss," he said silkily.

"Are you following me?" she asked in a whisper.

"Does the thought frighten you?"

"A little," she confessed.

"I'd like you to be a little afraid of me."

She turned to look at him. "Are you a dangerous man, Mr. Marino? Do I need to tell my husband about you?"

"I hope you don't tell him. It might make it more difficult to convince you to become my lover."

"You're quite bold, aren't you, Mr. Marino?"

"So I've been told."

"And a little ambiguous."

"How so, pretty lady?"

"I'm not sure if you wish to proposition me or frighten me."

"Why can't it be both?"

"You don't make any sense."

He leaned closer and whispered, "It's the sex."

Vera frowned in confusion.

"The sex, pretty lady. You'll find it more intense, more passionate if you have a healthy dose of fear. It's the unknown, the uncertainty you'll find addictive."

"I have no death wish." Vera turned abruptly and faced the window again.

Anthony laughed at her response. "Oh, trust me, princess, I've no intention of hurting you in that way. A little rough sex perhaps but nothing lethal. I've always taken good care of my toys. Rarely break them."

"Do you have any idea who I am?" Vera was both outraged and titillated at his words.

"Yes. You're the princess of Coulson, and you live in an ivory tower. I imagine you lead a very mundane life despite your husband's money. If you belonged to me—even temporarily—I wouldn't be satisfied putting you on some display shelf, where I simply looked and didn't touch. I'd be impatient to take you off the shelf, unwrap the package, and play with my favorite toy."

"I'm not a toy," Vera snapped.

"I'd like to make you mine. We'd have fun, Vera. I promise. I'll show you a good time, and when I have to leave in a few months, you can go back to your boring life, but at least you can remember what it was like to live life to the fullest for a short time."

"This is crazy talk. I need to go." Vera started to turn and walk away. Anthony reached out and took hold of her wrist.

Instead of pulling away, she looked down at the hand that held her.

"Wait, walk with me for a second. I want to show you something. I promise I won't hurt you. I don't want you if you aren't willing." He released his hold.

Against her better judgment, Vera followed Anthony down the sidewalk. They paused at the walkway leading to the restrooms.

"If you decide to take me up on my offer, just park your car along Main Street. Walk to the restrooms, and you can enter the back of the Cliffwood Motel through the trees. My room is number ten. It will be open. You're always welcome."

Without another word, he turned and walked in the opposite direction. Silently, Vera stood on the sidewalk, watching him get into a car and drive away. Nervously, she glanced up and down the street to see if anyone had seen her talking to Anthony Marino. There were less than a half dozen people on Main Street, and all were some distance away, and none seemed particularly interested in whom she had been talking with.

Instead of returning to her car or Mabel's Dress Boutique, Vera turned down the walkway leading to the restrooms. After using the facilities, she walked back outside and glanced at the rear of the building. Curious, she looked around to make sure she was alone, and then she walked toward the trees.

Pulling the branches to the side, she peeked through the limbs and looked at the back of the Cliffwood Motel. Hearing something, she glanced behind her. While looking at the building housing the restrooms, a hand reached between the trees and grabbed hold of her wrist. Before she knew what happened, she was yanked between the tree limbs and found herself standing on the sidewalk near room ten, with Anthony Marino.

"I didn't imagine you'd come so soon!" he said with a laugh.

"You scared me!" she snapped, brushing leaves from her sleeve.

"Sorry, love, I was just happy you came."

"I didn't come for you!" she insisted. "I had to use the restroom, and I was just curious to see. I never looked back here before."

"Well, you need to pay a toll if you want to return to the other side." Boldly, he wrapped his arms around her waist and pulled her close to him. She could feel the proof of his arousal pressing against her belly.

"Let me go," she hissed. "Or I'll scream!"

"And how will you explain why you're here?" He pulled her tighter. "One kiss and you can go. And you better hurry; the guy who runs this place is fixing a leak in room nine and is likely to walk out at any minute."

"Let me go!" She squirmed.

"One kiss, princess. And I want a real one. Then you can go."

Vera looked up into his dark eyes. She could tell by his stubborn expression he wasn't about to let her off without a kiss. How would she explain the situation if she was caught? *What would one kiss hurt?*

"Fine. One kiss. Then let me go," Vera said primly. Dropping her purse to the sidewalk, she wrapped her arms around his neck. *I'll show him a thing or two about kissing!*

Brazenly planting her lips on his, she boldly slipped her tongue in his mouth, intending to shock the man. Instead, her response fueled his desire, and before she could comprehend what was happening, his mouth ravaged hers.

Their tongues fenced, and heat rushed through Vera's limbs. She pulled him closer, succumbing to his dominance. She didn't resist when his right hand moved down her back and slipped to the front of her blouse, boldly capturing her left breast in his hand. He squeezed tightly, giving her a taste of how he liked to play rough.

Vera heard men talking, and it wasn't coming from the direction of the restrooms but from the motel. Abruptly she pushed Anthony from her, grabbed her purse off the ground, and made her hasty escape through the trees.

CHAPTER SEVEN

"I thought you were buying a new dress for tonight," Harrison asked when Vera entered the library. He and his father sat on the leather chairs, drinking scotch while waiting for Vera and Sonny to join them.

"You don't like this one?" Vera asked, glancing down at her dress as she took a seat on the small sofa.

"I didn't say that. I just thought you went shopping this afternoon."

"What's the point of buying last year's fashions? If you would let me take a trip to New York..."

"That's ridiculous," Randall scoffed. "Perfectly good clothes in Coulson."

"Where's Sonny?" Vera chose to ignore her father-in-law.

"He should be down soon." Harrison glanced at his watch. "Our reservation isn't for another thirty minutes; we have plenty of time."

"You haven't told me—you two seem to delight in keeping me in the dark. When will Sonny be leaving? I was hoping he'd be here for the holidays." Vera smoothed out imaginary wrinkles from her dress's skirt.

"He'll be here for your Halloween party, but don't count on him for Thanksgiving or Christmas. He's leaving right after the election," Randall told her.

"I don't know what the rush is," Vera said.

ANTHONY MARINO SAT ALONE IN HIS CAR, WATCHING. THIS was the most fun he'd had in months. She'd proved to be an easy and eager target. He had expected more resistance, but all he had to do was apply minimal pressure and she folded.

Headlights from the estate caught his attention, making their way down the long drive. When they reached the street, he saw it wasn't Vera's car but a limousine. Curious, he started his engine and followed from a discreet distance. When the limousine pulled into the Roseville parking lot, he turned into the gas station across the street. From the distance, it looked as if four people got out of the vehicle, aside from the chauffeur. He was fairly certain one of them was his princess. Anthony smiled. *Time to play*, he told himself.

THEY WERE JUST LOOKING AT THE MENU WHEN THE WAITRESS brought them a chilled bottle of expensive champagne, something they hadn't ordered.

"It's from a gentleman at the end of the bar," the server explained as she began to pour them each a glass. Wondering who their benefactor might be, they all turned toward the bar.

When Vera's gaze set on the man who was the subject of their curiosity, she froze. It was Anthony Marino. Sitting arrogantly at the end of the bar, his dark eyes watched for her reaction. The moment her eyes met his, a sly smile formed on his full lips. He stood up and began walking in her direction.

"Do we know him?" Harrison asked under his breath. Randall said nothing but watched with interest. Sonny seemed oblivious to the approaching man as he sipped the champagne, unconcerned as to its origin.

"Excuse me for intruding," Anthony said with a gallant flourish, making a brief bow. To all appearances, he was the perfect gentleman.

Vera was speechless, and while she had no idea what he was about to say, she couldn't take her eyes off him. There was something so—so—*sexy* about the man, in a very dangerous and forbidden way. She noticed his tailored suit immediately; it was not something he'd bought in Coulson. He might be brash, but the man knew how to dress.

All three Coulson men stood to greet Marino, and each accepted the hand offered when introductions were made.

"I'm Anthony Marino," he said as he shook Randall's hand before moving to greet Vera's husband.

"I'm Harrison Coulson; this is my wife, Vera, and our eldest son, Sonny. And my father, Randall. But I don't quite understand the champagne."

"Oh, please sit down. I only ask for a brief moment of your time," Anthony said after he had shaken their hands. The three Coulson men sat back down.

"I just wanted to send over the champagne as a thank you to your dear wife for being so tolerant of my boorish behavior."

"I'm afraid I don't understand." Harrison frowned.

"I happened to meet your wife the other day in Clement Falls. All very innocent, I assure you. We struck up a friendly conversation at the market, and I'm afraid I flirted shamefully with her. She immediately set me straight, informing me she was a married woman. I was, of course, devastated at that news. Yet, now in retrospect, I imagine I may have made her uncomfortable, and I wanted to apologize to her and to her husband."

"Are you the man who flirted with my mother?" Sonny blurted out.

"Sonny!" Vera gasped, horrified. Her face flamed red.

Anthony laughed. "Ah, she told you, then! Guilty. What I find difficult to believe is that she has a son your age. You look more like her younger brother." He then turned to Harrison. "You are a very lucky man, sir."

"Ah, you do love to flatter the ladies," Randall said. "Here, sit down and join us for a glass of the champagne you sent over."

"Thank you for the offer, but I don't wish to intrude. Enjoy your dinner...and the champagne." With a final bow, he returned to the bar.

"Randall, why did you invite him to sit down?" Vera asked.

"Does the man make you nervous?" Randall took a sip of his champagne.

"Well, we don't know anything about him."

"He's apparently quite smitten with you." Harrison grinned at Vera and then took a sip of the champagne.

Before Vera could respond, the waitress returned to the table to take their order. After she left, the conversation shifted from Anthony Marino to Sonny's European tour. Vera avoided looking in Anthony's direction. When she finally did, he was gone.

Vera found it difficult to focus on the evening's conversation. After she finished her dinner, she excused herself to go to the restroom. Leaving the men at her table in a heated discussion, they barely noticed her exit.

Walking from the dining room into the hallway, she glanced at her watch. It was almost 10 p.m. As she walked past the doorway leading to the lounge, she noticed there were only a few customers. She wondered if the late hour was the reason for the lack of people in the dining room and lounge.

The women's restroom was down a second hallway adjacent to the elevator. Once in the women's bathroom, she glanced under the stalls and didn't see any feet. She was alone. She took the first stall, and when she was done a few minutes later, she went to the sink to wash her hands. Just as she finished drying her hands, she heard the door to the restroom open and then heard footsteps.

She glanced toward the door. To her surprise, it was Anthony Marino. Vera watched in stunned silence as he locked the door so no one could enter. He then flashed a smile and walked in her direction.

"What are you doing?" she demanded, turning to face him.

"I wanted to see you," he said, his voice low.

She stepped back and her bottom hit the sink. "You can't be in here."

"I just wanted to say thank you."

"Thank you?"

"You kept our secret." He stopped walking and was a few feet from her.

Nervously, Vera smoothed the lines of her skirt. She glanced at the door and then back to Anthony. "I'm going to go now." She tried to step around him, but he blocked her way and grabbed her wrist. Her heart raced and she looked down at his hand as it held her in place.

"In a minute."

"What do you want?"

"I want to reward you for keeping our secret. I want to give you something special."

"I don't understand," she said nervously.

"Didn't I let you go after I kissed you? Give me a few minutes, and I'll let you go again."

"You want to kiss me again?" She felt dizzy.

"Not exactly. Turn around."

"What?"

"You heard what I said, turn around." When she didn't turn around fast enough to suit him, he reached out and placed his hands on her shoulders and turned her to face the mirror. Confused, she glanced over her shoulder at him.

"I want you to look in the mirror. I want you to watch."

"Watch what?" she asked, trembling. Instead of answering her, he stepped closer and wrapped his arms around her waist, holding her tightly. She began to struggle, but he held on tighter.

"Stop fighting or I'll let you go and I'll tell your husband how you kissed me—twice. How your tongue was down my throat. I wonder how your father-in-law will feel about that. And your son. What will he say when he learns his mother kisses strange men? I'll be convincing. And by your expression tonight, I doubt you'll be able to pull off a lie. And I won't be lying; your tongue was down my throat."

"What do you want from me?" Vera's head spun.

"I told you, I want to reward you for keeping our secret. Just relax, and you can return to your table in just a few minutes. I don't think this will take long."

His arms felt like steel bands holding her in place. She stopped struggling and closed her eyes.

"No," he whispered in her ear. "I want you to watch. Open your eyes."

With her heart pounding and her stomach churning, Vera opened her eyes and looked into the mirror. He was standing behind her, pressing his body against hers. Much taller than she was, he looked into the mirror, their eyes meeting.

Very slowly, he moved one of his hands down to her thigh and slipped it under the hem of her skirt. She gasped.

"Shh," he whispered into her ear. "This won't take long, and it'll feel good, I promise. Just relax." His hand moved all the way under her skirt. Boldly, he slipped his hand into her panties.

Looking into the mirror, she watched as her skirt hiked up. She could see her garter belt that held her nylons in place. He pulled her skirt up to her belly so he could see her panties.

"You're wet," he whispered into her ear, then nipped her earlobe.

Unable to move, she submitted to his touch. Expertly, his fingers played with her. Tugging her underwear down slightly, he could see the downy curls. He knew what stroke was needed, the precise amount of pressure to elicit the desired response. Anthony was right; it didn't take long.

When he brought her body to the desired conclusion, he held his fingers in her, relishing the prize. Before releasing her, he looked down at the damp curls at the juncture of her thighs. Low on her belly, just below her panty line, was a heart-shaped mole. His thumb moved over the mole as he nipped her neck. Finally, he moved his hand, straightened her underwear, and pulled the skirt of her dress back into place. Vera's glazed eyes looked back at him.

"I'll slip out the window; then you go back to your party."

"You can't go out the window. We're on the third floor."

"I have it covered. Don't worry about me, baby. I can't wait to take your clothes off when you come to my room."

"I can't go to your motel."

"Yes, you can."

Anthony grabbed her one last time, gave her a rough yet quick kiss, and then let her go. He walked to the window on the far wall, opened it, and climbed out, leaving Vera alone in the women's restroom.

Still dazed and confused, Vera walked to the window and looked out. The tree branches explained how he made it to the street.

On the way home from the restaurant, Vera was uncharacteristically quiet. Randall noticed a change in her demeanor after her visit to the restroom. Back at the house, the two Harrisons went upstairs, but Vera went to the kitchen to get a glass of water while Randall went into the library.

Heading upstairs, Vera passed the open library door.

"Vera," Randall called out. Pausing for a moment in the hallway, she considered ignoring him but changed her mind. She walked into the library.

"Yes, Randall?" She stood near the doorway.

"That man is dangerous. Stay away from him."

"Excuse me?" Vera couldn't believe he was talking about Anthony Marino. *He couldn't possibly know!*

"I saw how you two were looking at each other. If you have to take a lover, choose one you can control. You used to know how to do that."

"I don't know what you're talking about," she stammered.

"Yes, you do. When you got my son to marry you, you were calling the shots. There's too much at stake to get involved with someone like that."

"Like I said, I don't know what you're talking about. However, you were the one who invited him to sit with us."

"Yes, I did. You heard what I said. Stay away from him."

CHAPTER EIGHT

*R*estless and exhilarated, Anthony needed a drink. Bringing Coulson's reigning princess to climax while her clueless husband was down the hall gave him a rush. The men of Coulson might believe they're some big shots in this little shit town and that he was nothing but an out-of-town goon—but he knew. So did the princess. The look on her face was priceless when she stood there, taking it—enjoying it.

After leaving the Roseville parking lot, he drove straight to the liquor store. He needed to get there before it was closed, and buy a bottle of gin. The streets were fairly quiet. Even on a Friday night, the town was pretty dead. The only drivers on the road seemed to be high school students with late curfews. In the liquor store parking lot was one pickup truck, its bed filled with partying teenagers. The truck's driver had just gotten out of the cab and was now standing by the back of the vehicle, talking to those sitting in the truck bed.

Anthony's headlights flashed briefly on the driver as he pulled into the parking lot, making his way to a spot in front of the store. Immediately, he recognized the driver. It was the princess's middle son, Garret Coulson.

After she had caught his attention, he had gone digging for information on her and her family. He still found it hard to believe a babe with her body had given birth to three sons—especially considering the older one's age.

Anthony turned off his car's engine and got out of his vehicle. Garret turned to look at him, and Anthony knew instinctively what the kid wanted. *He wants me to buy him some booze.* Swaggering toward the truck on the way to the liquor store door, Anthony took his time and gave Garret a little nod in greeting. He figured the kid was trying to decide if he was safe to ask.

"How ya doing?" Garret greeted Anthony when he reached the truck. Anthony stopped by Garret and glanced at the teenagers in the back of the pickup.

"Doing great. You kids having fun?" Anthony flashed his most charming smile.

"Yeah, but it's a little dry tonight," Garret said, watching for Anthony's reaction.

"Need some beer, wine?"

"Hey, you'd do that?" Garret smiled.

"Hell yeah, I was young once." Anthony laughed.

Garret pulled some money out of his pocket and started to hand it to Anthony while telling him what they wanted.

"Come in with me and pick out what you want. That way you can carry it out."

"You sure?" Most guys who agreed to buy booze for him didn't want the checker in the liquor store to know what was going on.

"Yeah, no problem."

"My name's Garret." Garret offered his hand.

"Tony." The two shook hands and then walked inside the liquor store to buy booze.

When they returned to the truck ten minutes later, Garret tried to give Anthony extra money for buying the liquor.

"No, I don't want anything. Like I told you, I was young once."

"Well, thanks, man. That was really cool of you," Garret told him.

"No problem. I'm staying in town for a while, over at the Cliffwood. So if you ever get hard up for someone to buy, I'd be happy to help you out."

"Really? Thanks a lot."

"No problem. And have fun."

"THAT WAS REALLY COOL OF THE OLD DUDE," SHERYL TOLD Garret after they drove away, heading to a desolate cul-de-sac. The two were alone in the cab of the truck. With his left hand on the steering wheel and his other one on Sheryl's right shoulder, he pulled her closer to him as they drove down the dark road. His right hand wandered a bit, copping a quick feel. Instead of pushing his hand away, she giggled and snuggled closer.

"Did you bring some?" Sheryl asked.

"Some what?" Garret teased.

"You know what I mean. So we can do it."

Sheryl was just fifteen, and Garret hadn't been her first. But the girl loved to screw and he was more than willing to accommodate her. She wasn't his girlfriend, but she was always eager to get together at the last minute for some beer and sex. A petite little thing, she was not quite five feet three inches tall, with tiny breasts that could barely fill out an A-cup. A bottle blonde, she wore her thin hair long and her skirts short. He wouldn't call her pretty, but that didn't seem to matter in the dark.

The one thing Sheryl insisted on was that he wore a condom. He had no problem with that and no shortage of condoms. When he first hit puberty, his grandfather had called him in the library for a private talk.

"Do you like girls?" his grandfather had asked.

"Sure, yeah, I guess," Garret had responded.

"Do you want to see them naked? Do you think about touching their breasts?"

"Grandfather, please..." The question surprised and embarrassed Garret, yet he knew Randall Coulson well enough to understand that if the old man wanted to know something, he wouldn't stop until he had the desired answers. Finally, Garret answered truthfully.

"Yeah, I do. Can I go now?"

"No, we need to talk first. I should have had this talk with your father so your mother couldn't have tricked him."

"Tricked him?"

"That isn't important now; it all worked out. She gave me three grandsons. Your grandmother was only able to give me one son. So in retrospect, the one thing your father did right was have three sons, even though it wasn't his doing."

"I don't know what you're talking about." Garret was confused.

"Knowing how you are, Garret, you'll take any opportunity that comes your way to stick your pecker in some pussy. I just don't want you to be stupid about it. Here." His grandfather handed him a box of condoms. "Keep that thing covered before you go sticking it anywhere. I don't need you knocking up some girl, especially in Coulson. When it comes time to get married, you need to pick someone from the right family. A shotgun marriage might have worked for your father, but it probably won't for you, considering the type of girls you'll encounter here. Enjoy them all you want, but don't leave a baby in them."

It was then Garret had realized his mother had been pregnant with Sonny when his parents married. He had never really thought about it before, but when he considered Sonny's birthday and his parents' anniversary, it wasn't difficult to figure out.

From that time on, someone—probably someone from the household staff on his grandfather's orders—would periodically leave a box of condoms in his bathroom. He never suffered the embarrassment of trying to purchase them at the local pharmacy.

STREETS HAD BEEN CUT IN ON THE FAR SOUTH SIDE OF TOWN, but houses had not yet been built on the lots. Some of the streets were paved and some were dirt. Most of the lots were currently for sale by Coulson Enterprises' real estate division. A few had already been sold, yet were still bare land. Cul-de-sacs along this area of Coulson had become a popular party spot for the bored teenagers of the small town.

Garret parked the truck and got out with Sheryl. They could hear voices and music coming from nearby cul-de-sacs, from other teenage partiers. He grabbed a blanket and a six-pack of beer from the back of the truck and walked with Sheryl to an isolated spot away from the vehicle. The three couples in the truck bed had hopped out when Garret first parked and had headed out in opposite directions to find their own dark corners.

One thing Garret liked about Sheryl, she didn't care about all that preliminary bullshit some of the girls expected. No reason to sweet-talk her or buy her gifts. After downing several beers, Sheryl removed her clothes. Garret didn't bother removing his; he just unbuttoned his denims and put on a condom.

When Garret was finished, he rolled off Sheryl, his breathing labored. Removing the condom, he tossed it into the dirt, tucked his penis back in his shorts, and zipped up his pants. Sheryl sat up and started to put her clothes back on.

"Did you leave your cigarettes in the truck?" she asked as she redressed.

"I have some in my shirt," Garret told her. He looked up at the stars as he took the pack of cigarettes out of his shirt pocket. "But I think you smashed them."

"Well, you could've taken your clothes off. I removed mine."

The package was slightly squished, but the cigarettes remained intact. Garret removed two cigarettes and lit one, then handed it to Sheryl. He lit the second one for himself and continued to lie on the blanket, staring up at the stars.

"Why? You got where you needed to go," he said.

"I know, but still. I think it's only fair you take your clothes off too." Sitting on the blanket, she took a drag off the cigarette.

They sat in silence for a few moments before Sheryl asked, "What are you doing the Saturday before Halloween? Suzie's having a party. Her folks are going to Vegas that weekend."

"My mother's having one of her parties that night. I'm

supposed to be there. I plan to cut out as soon as I can make my escape."

"A costume party?" Sheryl asked.

"I guess."

"Can you take a date?"

"To the party?"

"Yeah."

"If I wanted to. Which I don't." Garret tossed his cigarette butt in the direction he had pitched the used condom.

"Take me, Garret. Please. I'd love to see inside your house," Sheryl pleaded.

Garret sat up. "Sheryl, I've always been straight with you. We aren't dating. You aren't my girlfriend."

"I know," she said sadly.

Garret stood up. "Let's get out of here."

"So soon?" She remained sitting on the blanket. The moonlight and stars above provided the only illumination.

"If you want to go another round, I'm up for it," Garret suggested. He dug into his pocket and pulled out another condom.

"So you really won't take me to the costume party?"

"No. What do you want to do? You want me to take you home, or do you want to do it again?"

Sheryl didn't answer immediately. After a few moments of silence, she began removing her clothes. Garret unzipped his pants and returned to the blanket.

VERA LEFT RANDALL IN THE LIBRARY, AND SHE WENT UP TO her bedroom. On her way down the hall, she glanced in Harrison's room. They hadn't shared a bedroom since Russell's birth.

She had taken a shower before dinner, so getting ready for bed took her less than fifteen minutes. Exhausted, she climbed in between her clean sheets and fell asleep.

"Fanny, come here to your Charles," Fred beckoned.

She knew what he expected of her. "Do we have to, Fred?"

Vera was always frightened when he initiated the play. It hurt so much the first time. But then—then she came to enjoy the pain and the pleasure.

"Don't call me Fred. Remember, I'm Charles, and who are you?"

"I'm your Fanny," she said obediently.

"Good girl. Remember how I saved you from that horrible man?"

"I guess..." Fanny stammered.

"Vera, do I have to read that part again to you?"

"No!" She hated that part of the book. The man in the story reminded her of her music teacher.

Obediently, she stood very still while he lifted her skirts and pulled down her underwear.

"Hold your skirt up for me, Fanny, so I can see."

Together they looked in the mirror and watched while his fingers toyed with the hidden folds. Looking down, she wondered where her curls had gone, and then she remembered she didn't have them yet. Glancing up, it was no longer Fred's face nor Charles's face, it was Anthony's.

It felt good—it always did—but then he—Charles, no Fred —or was it Anthony?—pushed her down on the floor and used his hard shaft instead of fingers, hammering into her until she exploded into a million colorful pieces.

CHAPTER NINE

"*I* really don't want to go to church with you tomorrow," Sonny told his parents and grandfather Saturday evening at supper. The family sat around the dinner table at Coulson House. Garret was the only absent family member.

"It's nonnegotiable," Randall told his grandson. Sonny's parents said nothing, but listened to the exchange.

"Well, Grandfather, I'm an adult now. A college graduate. If I don't want to attend church, that should be my prerogative."

"Fine," Randall said as he took a roll from the breadbasket and tore it in half.

"Fine? Then you're okay with it?" Sonny asked.

"No. But I can't make you go. As you said, you're an adult now." Randall took a bite of his roll. "Of course, I imagine an adult can pay for his own European tour."

"Are you saying I can't go on the trip if I refuse to go to church with you?"

"Certainly not. You're free to go to Europe. You're an adult. But I don't have to pay for it."

Sonny sat dumbly at the table, saying nothing.

"Dad, did you go to church when you were a kid?" Russell asked his father.

"No, we didn't start going to church until I married your mother."

"Your father's right," Randall said. "Your grandmother and I never attended church. My family was Baptist. When I left home, I swore I'd never go back. As for your grandmother, I can't remember what church her family attended. But she stopped going when we were married."

"Grandfather, I would think you'd understand my feelings, considering you stopped going to church when you left home," Sonny said.

Randall set his fork on the table and looked at his eldest grandson. "You say you're an adult, Sonny. It's time you realize there are certain things we must do—for both business and political reasons."

"Political?" Sonny asked.

"Yes. The future is unlimited for the men in this family. There may come a time we want to test the waters of politics, but before we do, we need to present the perfect image of the American family. The perfect American family attends church together on Sundays."

"I'll go, Grandfather," Sonny begrudgingly conceded. It was quiet for a few minutes at the dinner table as everyone ate. Finally, Sonny asked, "Does Garret go to church with the family?" Sonny couldn't imagine his brother would still be attending church every Sunday.

Vera looked up at Sonny and gave a sardonic smile. "Much to the minister's chagrin," she said.

"I don't understand?" Sonny frowned.

"How old was Garret when you left for college? Twelve?

I don't think you appreciate your younger brother's personal charm," Randall said.

"I don't know why you find it so amusing." Vera sounded annoyed. She looked over at her eldest son. "Garret is out of control and your father and grandfather find it amusing."

"Oh, he isn't that bad," her husband said. "He's just a typical teenage boy, sowing his wild oats."

"I still don't understand why you said *much to the minister's chagrin*," Sonny asked.

"Some very *nice* girls attend our church," Vera explained. "From very nice families. Garret seems to delight in flirting with—and sitting with these young girls at church, and it's fairly obvious it makes their parents uncomfortable."

"The girls really like Garret," Russell said.

———

ANTHONY WAS GETTING RESTLESS. HE FIGURED IT WAS TIME TO step up the game. He hadn't seen the princess since Friday night. He had driven by her house several times on Saturday but didn't venture up the long drive to the estate or park on the street.

Cruising around town on Sunday morning, he noticed the Coulson limousine at one of the churches. He parked across the street for an hour and just watched. When services were over, he saw them—the princess and her family. *I wonder if she confessed her sins*, he asked himself with a chuckle. Then he remembered protestant churches didn't have confessionals, at least that was what he understood.

Anthony watched as she got into the limo with the old man, her husband and oldest son. He recognized Garret, who was with a small boy. Instead of getting into the limo, the two were walking over to Garret's truck. Anthony remembered she had a third son about this boy's age. Taking a pair of binoculars out of the glove compartment, he took a closer look.

Good-looking boy, he thought. He didn't think it was fair that her husband had three strapping boys and a hot wife. Especially considering the fact Coulson wasn't giving the woman what she clearly needed. There was no way she would have responded the way she did in the bathroom if she wasn't starving for a man's touch. Another woman might have submissively let him have his way, but there would have been tears. There were no tears with the princess—just soaked panties.

It wasn't difficult to follow the limousine without being seen, considering the number of cars leaving the church parking lot at the same time. When they pulled up to a restaurant a couple of miles away, he figured they were going to have breakfast. Knowing women, he knew where he would find her.

Anthony slipped into the back entrance of the restaurant and located the women's restroom. He stood by the door for a moment, waiting to see if anyone was coming out. Finally, a woman exited.

"Excuse me," he asked the woman. "I'm looking for my wife, and I think she went in the lady's room. Was a redhead in there?"

"No. There isn't anyone in there," the woman told him. Anthony thanked her and watched her walk away. When no one was looking, he slipped into the women's restroom. He was pleased to discover a storage room off the bathroom. The door was locked, but it took him less than a minute to get it open and slip inside.

The storage room was even larger than he had expected.

It would easily hold two people. Keeping the door slightly ajar, he could see who was coming into the bathroom.

She arrived even sooner than he had anticipated. The princess was alone.

Vera was about to walk into the first stall when a hand from the storage room reached out and grabbed her while a second hand covered her mouth. In the next moment, she found herself in a dark closet, held captive by a pair of strong arms.

"Settle down, princess," the voice whispered. She knew instantly who it was. Vera did as she was told.

"Please, let me go," she whispered.

"I just needed to see you. I missed you. You're so beautiful, you know. I won't hurt you."

"Please just let me go. I won't say anything."

"I know you won't, princess, because you know we're meant for each other. I can give you what you need. A woman like you needs special care."

"Please, I'll scream."

"No, you won't. If you do, I'll tell your husband you came willingly."

"He won't believe you," she whispered.

"He will when I tell him how I know you have a sexy little heart-shaped mole."

"Please…" Vera began to shake.

"Princess, if you didn't want this, didn't need this, you would have screamed by now. You need what I can give you."

"No…" She trembled.

"Baby, your husband isn't man enough for a woman like you. When was the last time he gave you what you needed? Gave you what I gave you Friday night?"

"What do you want from me?" she asked.

Instead of answering her question, he showed her. Anthony's mouth claimed hers while his arms wrapped around her, holding her close.

Vera could not remember the last time she had been kissed like this. She had only been with two men in her entire life. The first was a neighbor—Fred, the husband to one of her mother's best friends. She was only fourteen at the time and still a virgin. Vera never told her mother—or anyone what had happened.

When Anthony kissed her—demanded she acquiesce— she was that fourteen-year-old girl again, submitting from fear, confusion, and conflicting sexual desire. Anthony intuitively knew he was in control, that she would do whatever he asked.

Without saying a word, he pushed Vera to her knees and unzipped his pants.

VERA STOOD AT THE SINK AND LOOKED INTO THE MIRROR. Anthony had slipped out of the bathroom a few minutes earlier, and there were two women in the stalls. They had entered when she was still in the closet with Anthony—on her knees.

Terrified that they would hear them or open the door, she submissively followed Anthony's silent instructions. She could still taste him. Had she not followed his instructions exactly, her Sunday dress would now be spattered with his seed. She felt ill.

Trembling, she washed her face with a paper towel.

"I WAS JUST GOING TO COME BACK TO CHECK ON YOU," Harrison said when she returned to the table. He then took a closer look and frowned. "Vera, are you all right? You look all flushed, and you've been crying."

"I'm afraid I'm sick." It wasn't a complete lie. "I'm going to have the driver take me home. You stay here and enjoy your breakfast."

"Are you sure?" Randall asked.

"Yes. It's just a bad headache. Sometimes those make me ill."

On the ride back home, Vera sat alone in the back of the limousine, lost in private thought. Closing her eyes, she visualized herself on her knees before Anthony.

For as long as she could remember, she was simply going through the motions. It wasn't just that she was not happy—she felt nothing. While a part of her was repulsed over what Anthony had made her do in the storage room, he'd also made her feel something.

By feeling something, she once again felt alive. *A moth to flame*, she thought.

CHAPTER TEN

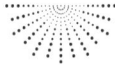

*G*arret took Russell home after church and then left to find his friends. Russell dashed upstairs to his room, changed his clothes, and came back downstairs again to go outside. He got onto his black Stingray bicycle and coasted down the long drive leading to the street. It gave him enough momentum so that he didn't have to pedal right away. He was planning to meet Ryan Keller for a game of over-the-line. But first, he'd stop at Tommy's to see if he wanted to join them.

He didn't know if the family was home or perhaps at an afternoon church service. When he reached Tommy's street, he noticed a station wagon in the driveway. It looked like someone was home. After reaching the Chamberlain's house, he dropped his bike in the driveway next to the car, rushed up to the front door, and rang the bell.

"Hi, Russell," Tommy greeted him when he opened the door.

"Hey, Tommy. The other day you said you're going back to school tomorrow, so I wondered if you wanted to go to the park to play over-the-line."

"Do you have two other guys?" Tommy asked.

"Yeah, Mike and Ryan from our class."

"Sure, let me go ask my mom." Tommy ran into the house, leaving the door open. Russell waited outside.

Beth Chamberlain gave Tommy permission to ride into town with Russell. Standing on the front porch, she watched the two boys pedal away, Tommy on his battered red Stingray and Russell on his shiny black one.

They met Ryan Keller at the motel, then rode down to the nearby park. Ryan's little brother, Jimmy, tagged along, riding his bike. An Indian summer afternoon, they played ball for about two hours. Mike was the first one to head home after the game. Tommy sat with Russell and Ryan on the grass while Jimmy climbed a nearby tree.

"Glad my mom let me come. That was fun," Tommy said.

"You're coming back to school tomorrow?" Ryan asked.

"Yeah. I might as well go to school; they make me do the stupid homework anyway."

"I don't like staying home," Russell said.

"Gee, why not? Your house looks neat. Like a haunted house," Ryan said.

Russell only shrugged.

"Oh yeah, where is that?" Tommy asked.

"He lives in the biggest house in Coulson. Bigger than our motel!" Ryan exclaimed.

"No way. I've seen the biggest house in town, up on that hill with that long steep driveway."

"That's it," Ryan told him.

Tommy turned to look at Russell. "Really?"

Russell shrugged again. "Yeah. But there's no one to hang out with. They never have any stickball games on our street like over on Mike's, and I can't just walk to town, like from Ryan's. My brothers are too old to hang out with. Garret is usually pretty cool, like when he drives me to school and tells Sonny to leave me alone. But it isn't like we hang out or anything."

"Well, Ryan's lucky to have a brother instead of two little sisters. They just want to play dolls and have stupid tea parties."

WHEN ANTHONY PULLED INTO THE PARKING LOT AT THE motel, he noticed four little boys on bicycles. He immediately recognized two of them; they were Keller's kids. After he first moved in, he'd made friends with the boys, giving them each a candy bar. He explained that when he was at the motel, he needed to sleep and that he was a really light sleeper. If they could keep far away from the door, he would reward them with candy.

"Our dad really doesn't like us to eat candy," Jimmy had told him. Ryan had given his little brother a sock and told him one candy bar was no big deal.

Anthony had laughed and said, "I like how this kid thinks. How about we keep this between us? Our secret. You boys keep away from my side of the motel, and I'll make sure someone leaves two candy bars in the mailbox each morning."

Ryan loved the idea, and Jimmy had to agree, who could argue with free candy bars? Before they left for school each day, the brothers raced to the mailbox, grabbed their candy bars, and rode off to school. They thought Anthony Marino was a really cool guy, and they never went over to his side of the motel.

"Hi, boys, been playing ball?" Anthony greeted them

after he got out of his Lincoln Continental. He had noticed the ball and mitt in the basket of Ryan's bike.

"Hi, Mr. Marino!" Jimmy greeted him. "They wouldn't let me play, but I watched."

"Jimmy, before long they'll be asking you to play." Anthony gave him a little wink then glanced at the other two boys. There was something familiar about the blond one with the blue eyes. The boys were now walking their bikes.

"So who are your friends?" he asked with a smile.

"This is Tommy and Russell," Jimmy explained. "They're in Ryan's class at school."

As he had been taught, Russell offered Anthony his hand. "Hi, I'm Russell Coulson."

"Coulson?" Anthony smiled; recognition dawned. "I know your parents."

"You do?"

"Not well, but we've met. Have fun, boys." Anthony lingered by his car while the boys walked their bikes toward the motel. He listened to their conversation.

"I got to head home soon," Tommy said.

"Me too," Russell said.

"Can't you come in?" Ryan asked. "We have cookies."

"I can stay for cookies," Tommy said.

"Yeah, me too, but I can't stay long," Russell agreed.

They pushed their bikes to a patch of dirt by the motel and dropped them. Running into the motel office, Ryan led the way to the kitchen in the residential portion of the motel for a snack.

"So how was the game?" Wally Keller asked.

"It was fun," Ryan told his father.

"They wouldn't let me play," Jimmy said.

"But they let you go along." Wally gave his youngest son's hair a quick ruffle. "Who were you boys talking to outside?"

"Mr. Marino. He's nice," Jimmy said.

"You boys know you aren't supposed to bother the guests."

"We didn't. He said hello first," Ryan explained.

"And remember, you are never to go to their rooms with them. If one even suggests it, you are to come tell me, remember?"

"Oh, Mr. Marino likes us to stay away from his room," Jimmy told his father. Ryan punched his arm when their father wasn't looking. He didn't want Jimmy to let it slip about the candy.

"He told us he likes quiet and asked us not to play over there," Ryan added.

"Well, that's good, I suppose." Wally had to admit Anthony Marino was the model motel guest. He never complained, and he paid in advance. While he was friendly, he never hung out in the office, wanting to chat. Wally wondered if Marino intended to move to Coulson full-time when—or if—any of his business deals panned out.

The three older boys took their snacks into Ryan and Jimmy's bedroom and shut the door. Jimmy stayed in the living room with his father and watched cartoons.

"What are you guys doing for Halloween?" Ryan asked as he hopped up on the top bunk and looked down at his friends.

"Dad always takes us trick-or-treating while Mom stays home and hands out candy. I really don't want to go with them this year. My sisters always wear something apey, like princess costumes."

"Then come over here on Halloween. I heard some of the stores are handing out candy, and the guy at the bike shop is setting up a haunted house," Ryan told him.

"That sounds cool," Russell said.

"I was thinking of going as a pirate, but I think I'd rather be something scary," Tommy said.

"Me too. My brother's going as a cowboy. I'd only be a cowboy if I was all bloody, like I was shot in a gunfight."

Tommy and Russell agreed; a bloody cowboy would be much cooler than what Jimmy wanted to wear.

BACK AT HIS MOTEL ROOM, ANTHONY SAT AT A RICKETY DESK. Earlier that day, he had stopped at the dime store and picked up some paper and envelopes. His plan was to write the princess a letter and put it in the mail. But this was even better; he would have her son deliver the letter.

Putting pen to paper, Anthony began to write. When he was finished, he allowed the ink to dry before folding the piece of paper neatly in half and slipping it into an envelope. Sealing the envelope, he looked at it a moment and smiled.

Leaving his motel room, he walked to the parking lot and leaned against his car, waiting for Russell Coulson. Anthony was still hanging out by his car when Russell and Tommy picked up their bikes to go home. As they headed toward the street, Anthony walked from his parked car to Russell.

"I was wondering if you could do me a favor," Anthony asked.

Russell looked up curiously.

"I mentioned I know your parents. Actually, your

mother is trying to arrange a surprise for your father. I think I know where she can get what she's looking for, so I was hoping you could give her this note."

Russell looked at the envelope Anthony was handing him. Hesitantly, he took it; it was sealed. He looked up at the man.

"But please, give it to your mother and don't let anyone see it. No one. If you do, well, that might ruin your mother's surprise. You wouldn't want to do that, would you?"

Holding the envelope, Russell thought of his mother. He was always trying to do little things to gain her favor, but nothing ever seemed to work. Smiling, Russell liked the idea of keeping his mother's secret.

"Sure," Russell said brightly. "And I promise I won't let anyone else see it, not even my brother Garret."

"Good. I'm sure that will make your mother happy. And after you give it to her, if you feel funny about keeping a secret from your dad, make sure you ask your mother first if you can tell him or your grandpa or anyone about me and the letter. You wouldn't want to do anything to upset your mom."

Russell again promised to keep the secret. Tucking the letter in his pocket, he rode off with Tommy and headed home.

VERA COULSON SAT ALONE IN THE LIBRARY, READING A magazine. After brunch, the two Harrisons and Randall went golfing. They still were not home.

Setting the magazine on her lap, she thought of Anthony Marino. The man terrified her, but he also excited her. Men gave her compliments, but Anthony made her believe them.

He didn't see her as a middle-aged mother, but as a woman he couldn't keep his hands off.

Vera knew her father-in-law was a rich and powerful man. But Anthony Marino was willing to risk discovery— even to the extent of telling on himself—to be with her. Having someone want her so strongly was a powerful aphrodisiac. It had been that way with Fred. Unable to handle his desire for Vera, he had eventually taken his own life.

She heard footsteps running down the hall and assumed Russell was home. Sighing, she picked up the magazine and began to read again.

Russell dashed into the library, slightly out of breath. "Mom, I was looking for you!"

Vera set her magazine down and looked at Russell. "Well, here I am; what do you want?"

"Are you alone?" He looked around the room.

"Of course I'm alone. Can't you see that?" she said impatiently.

"Someone gave me a secret note for you, and I can't tell anyone. Just you!" He dug into his pocket and pulled out the now crumpled envelope. He handed it to his mother.

Wrinkling her nose, she accepted it. Absently opening the envelope, she asked, "What is this?"

Instead of answering, Russell let her read the letter.

WE NEED TO CONCLUDE OUR TRANSACTION. THIS MORNING YOU *got a taste of what I am looking for. You know the meeting place. Be there noon tomorrow. Give my regards to your husband and father-in-law. I will be contacting them shortly to discuss your mole—unless you can convince me otherwise when we meet.*

"Where did you get this?" Vera demanded. She sounded mad, which confused Russell.

"A man gave it to me," Russell explained. He hadn't expected her to react this way. "Did I do something wrong?"

"Where did you meet him?"

"I was at Ryan Keller's. His dad owns that motel near the hobby shop. The man is staying at the motel. Did I do something wrong?"

"What did he say to you?" Vera was clearly agitated.

"He said you were trying to surprise Dad with something, and he knew where you might get what you needed. He said I was not to tell anyone about the note but you. Should I tell Dad?"

Vera reached out to Russell and clutched his hand. "No, dear," she said quickly, forcing a smile. "You did the right thing. Yes...yes...the man was correct. I'm planning a surprise for your father. We mustn't tell anyone. It will be our little secret."

Vera gathered Russell into her arms and gave him a hug.

CHAPTER ELEVEN

*G*arret left for school early on Monday morning. His
first class didn't start for almost an hour, but he
had promised Russell he would give him a ride so
the third grader didn't have to take the bus.

Walking toward the library, he noticed three upper-
classmen at the side of the gym with Sheryl. Glancing over,
it appeared she was trying to walk away, but the boys had
formed a circle around her and wouldn't let her leave.

After their date on Friday night, he saw her again
Saturday evening when he stopped at Burger Shack to grab
something to eat with friends. She was sitting in a car with a
couple of guys from the football team, so he didn't talk to
her. He figured she was a free agent and didn't give her
much thought. But now, she didn't look happy. Changing
route, he walked toward Sheryl and the boys. He recognized
them. They were all seniors, members of the football team,
and a year older than him: Stu Parker, Craig Mason, and
Richard Brown.

"Hey, what's going on?" Garret asked as he approached.
Startled, the boys looked in his direction. They hadn't seen

him coming. Sheryl took the opportunity to rush to Garret's side.

"Please get me out of here," she pleaded in a whisper. Garret studied her face; she had been crying.

Now angry, Garret pushed Sheryl behind him, blocking her from the football players as he faced the three boys.

"What the hell is going on?" Garret demanded.

"No big deal," Stu insisted. A bit uneasy with Garret's sudden interest, Stu shifted nervously. Stu's dad worked in the local Coulson factory, and his old man would kill him if he and his friends did something to Garret Coulson. While Stu didn't think he could take Garret himself, he knew he could with his two friends.

"We were just arranging a little fun with Sheryl. Everyone knows how she loves a good gang bang," Richard said.

"What did you say?" Garret seethed and moved closer, his hands balling into fists.

"Oh, come on, Coulson, the whole school knows she's just a slut. What's the big deal? Even you've been getting some of it, so don't act like you don't know," Craig said.

Without hesitation, Garret lurched forward and punched Craig in the face. The boy fell to the ground. Richard and Stu did not rush to defend their friend but stood silently.

"Leave her alone. If I hear you guys have been talking trash about her again—or if you lay a hand on her again—you will hear from me."

Rubbing his injured jaw, Craig stood up and mumbled something under his breath. The three boys made their hasty departure.

Garret turned to Sheryl. Tears streamed down her face.

He gathered her in his arms and held her for a moment, letting her cry. Finally the sobs subsided.

"They'll leave you alone now," he promised.

"They were right. I'm the joke around here."

Garret sighed and then released her, looking again into her face. With one hand, he wiped away her tears.

"Sheryl, you're a good person. Don't let those assholes get to you. Hell, you aren't doing anything they aren't."

"But they're guys."

"Yeah, I guess we can get away with more shit. You just need to avoid assholes like that. Pick guys who don't treat you like crap."

"Like you?" she whispered, faintly hopeful.

"I like you, Sheryl. And I promise I never talk shit behind your back. But I don't want you to get the wrong impression. There will never be anything between us aside from friendship and some fun. If you want more, then maybe we shouldn't get together again. But even if we don't, I want you to know I'll still consider you my friend."

"Garret, when's your next class?" She was no longer crying.

He glanced at his watch. "Forty five minutes, why?"

"I thought we could get the hell out of here for a while before your first class. That is, if you have any condoms in your truck."

"You don't have to do that."

"I know." Sheryl smiled up at Garret. "But I want to."

The two walked out to his truck. After they climbed into the cab, he reached over and opened his glove compartment. It was empty.

"Fuck," Garret cursed. "I don't have any."

"That's okay," Sheryl said, placing her hand on his thigh.

"No, it's not. My grandfather would kill me."

"I mean, there are other ways. Come on, I want to. What I have in mind, I can't get pregnant."

Garret looked at her. He wondered if she meant what he thought. Sheryl smiled adoringly at Garret.

"Please, Garret. Let me do this for you. I want to show you how much I appreciate what you did back there."

Somewhere in the back of Garret's mind was a small voice telling him it was wrong to take Sheryl up on her offer. She was vulnerable and would probably do whatever he asked. But the horny sixteen-year-old shut out the voice and put the key in the ignition.

He drove to a nearby park and stopped in a desolate area. They didn't even have to get out of the vehicle. It was over pretty quickly, and since Sheryl hadn't removed any of her clothes, she didn't need to redress. The girl had some pretty impressive oral skills, and she left no evidence of the deed on his clothes or the seat.

Garret drove back to the high school with a smile on his face and a twinge of guilt tugging on his conscience.

BETH CHAMBERLAIN SAT AT THE BACK OF THE CLASSROOM, watching her students work quietly at their desks. She had just finished grading the test papers from last Friday and she was very pleased, especially with Garret Coulson's test.

"Mr. Coulson, would you please come here for a moment?" she called out. Garret stopped working on his algebra assignment and glanced towards the teacher at the back of the room. Setting his pencil down, he stood up and walked towards her.

"Yes?" Garret stood by the teacher's desk.

Beth looked up at Garret and smiled. "I just wanted to let

you know I finished correcting the tests from last Friday. You were the only one who scored one hundred percent. Congratulations."

Garret shrugged and said, "It was an easy test."

"No. I don't believe that's it at all. Perhaps it was easy—for you. But no easier than the other two tests we've had so far this year. The difference, in my opinion, is you didn't rush and you took the entire time allotted to take the test. I noticed with the first two, you whizzed through them both, turned them in after fifteen minutes, and while you passed the tests, you only got a C on each one. Garret, if you keep this up, I see no reason why you can't get an A in this class."

"Well, I just figured I didn't have anywhere else to go, so I might as well work a little longer on the test."

Beth smiled at Garret, delighted he was actually trying. "You know, Garret, I see no reason why you can't do as well in all your other classes. I'm very proud of you. I just wanted you to know that."

"How's your daughter doing?" Garret asked, abruptly changing the subject. Beth suspected he was uncomfortable with praise.

"Alexandra? Why, she's doing very well, thank you. Although, I suspect those little boys who were chasing her are still having nightmares."

Garret chuckled. "It serves them right for picking on a little girl."

"By the way, I met your younger brother. He's in my son's class."

"Yeah, Russell mentioned something about that to me. He's a good kid. You don't have to worry about your son hanging out with him. Russell isn't anything like me. Kid always gets good grades, never gets in scrapes."

"Well, Garret, from what I understand, you never get in trouble at school." Beth eyed him with curiosity.

Garret leaned closer to the desk. "Mrs. Chamberlain, you know why that is. If I was anyone else, I'd be racking up hours in detention. Most people around here are afraid to reprimand me. Everyone but you." He flashed Beth his most charming smile, then headed back to his desk.

CHAPTER TWELVE

*L*ike a child terrified to go into the haunted house yet
unable to resist, Vera found herself walking toward
the public restrooms off Main Street. She didn't go
immediately to the row of trees behind the building, but
instead went into the lady's room and looked into the
mirror.

She had parked her car down the street, in front of the
hobby shop. It wasn't quite noon yet. Glancing at her watch,
she had five more minutes. When she left home that morning, only the household staff was on the premises. Sonny
had gone to the office with his father and grandfather.

Her husband never asked her where she was going or
when she might be home. She doubted he really cared. Vera
wasn't stupid. She knew her husband had a lover. What she
didn't know—had he started seeing other women before she
sent him from her bed or after?

Looking in the mirror, she brushed her fingers through
her hair and straightened her dress. Placing her hand on the
middle of her chest, she held it there for a moment. It
reminded her of a drum, the way her rapid heartbeat

vibrated the palm of her hand. She had never been so nervous in her entire life. Terrified and exhilarated—one emotion fed the other. Glancing at her watch, she knew it was time. She needed to go. She had no choice. Vera wasn't sure she wanted one.

Walking out of the restroom building, she looked around. There was no one on the walkway and the building was not visible from the street. Hastily, she made her way to the trees. Pushing the branches to one side, she saw room ten's door.

Slipping quickly between the branches so no one would see her should they walk down the sidewalk to the restrooms from the shops, she made her way to room ten. She heard voices. Someone was coming down the walkway of the motel, and if she didn't do something quick, they would see her standing there.

ANTHONY LOUNGED LAZILY ON HIS HOTEL BED, LEANING against the headboard as his legs stretched out on the mattress. He wore just a robe with nothing underneath. Glancing at his watch, he noted it was a few minutes before noon.

He had left the door unlocked and the windows and curtains closed. The lamp next to the bed provided the only lighting.

Seconds after he checked the time, the door burst open and Vera rushed in, slamming the door behind her. She leaned against the door as if someone was after her. He watched as she looked around the room, her eyes adjusting to the light.

"Why did you slam the door?" Anthony asked, slightly amused.

"Someone was out there. I heard voices."

"Then lock it if you want, put on the latch. And come here."

Obediently, Vera locked the door, fastening the latch so even someone with a key would not be able to enter. After securing the door, she approached the bed.

Anthony did not move but enjoyed watching Vera from the comfort of the bed. She seemed nervous, but she was following his instructions. When she was by the foot of the bed, she paused, as if uncertain what to do now.

"Vera, have you ever stepped out on your husband?" Anthony asked.

"No," she whispered.

"You've never been unfaithful to him?"

"Never."

Anthony was pleased with her answer. He believed her. It made her a much more valuable piece in his estimation.

"When was the last time you had sex with your husband?"

The question startled Vera, and she just stood there, not responding.

"Please answer my question." His voice was stern.

"Before Russell was born."

The answer surprised Anthony. He sat up straighter in the bed. *Did her husband not like women?* "Why?" he asked.

"I...I told him I didn't want him anymore," she confessed.

"And he simply accepted that? The man is a fool. Take off your dress, princess. I want you to strip for me."

Vera's eyes widened.

"Do it, princess, now. You'll discover I'm nothing like your husband. You belong to me now. Take it off."

He watched as her trembling hands reached back awkwardly and unzipped the dress. She pulled it over her head and folded it neatly, setting it on the desk chair. He chuckled to himself, finding such tidy behavior amusing.

She stood there a moment, concealed by her slip and bra. Nervously she removed her shoes but stopped there.

"The rest, princess. I want it all off for the first time. Perhaps the next time you come, don't wear any panties, that way you can leave your garters and nylons on."

"Next time?"

"Yes. Like I said, you belong to me now. Take the rest off and get your ass over here. I'm getting impatient."

When Vera was completely nude, she nervously made her way to the bed. Anthony stood up for a moment and removed his robe, tossing it carelessly to the floor. She could not take her eyes from Anthony's nude body. His broad chest looked as if it were covered with a thick blanket of fur. Even his muscular thighs were covered with black hair. His penis jutted out, already engorged, much larger than her husband's. There was something terrifying—intimidating about Anthony's nude body.

She did not have time to think about it, for in the next moment he grabbed her by the wrist and tossed her onto the bed. Climbing on, Anthony wasted no time getting exactly what he wanted from Vera Coulson. He was not gentle with his lovemaking and used her roughly. In spite of his roughness, he made sure she climaxed.

LYING QUIETLY NEXT TO ANTHONY, VERA SAID NOTHING AS HE

smoked a cigarette while using his free hand to stroke her left breast. She looked up to the ceiling, trying to comprehend all that had happened.

"Can you still get pregnant?" he asked while smashing his cigarette into the ashtray on the nightstand.

"Pregnant?" Vera asked dumbly.

"Well, my sister can't anymore. She had a kid, and something happened so she can't get pregnant again. I wondered, you have three kids, anything happen where you can't get knocked up?"

"I...I...hadn't considered. It took me a long time to get pregnant with our last one. I don't know."

Anthony chuckled. He moved his hand down from her breast and rubbed her stomach. "Who knows, maybe I'll put a baby in your belly. What do you think your tight-ass husband would think of that?"

He massaged her stomach even harder. "I might just get me another son." Anthony rolled over on Vera, and without any foreplay, he took her again.

"What time is good for you tomorrow?" Anthony reclined on the bed, watching Vera as she redressed.

"Tomorrow?" she asked numbly.

"I'm not unreasonable. I don't expect you to come every day at noon. So what is the best time for you tomorrow?"

"I can't come here tomorrow." Vera's hands trembled.

"You didn't hear me, princess. I own you. You tell me what time, or I'll tell you."

"I can't do this again. I might get pregnant."

Anthony laughed. "Who knows, maybe you are now. Okay, be here at noon tomorrow."

"No."

"Princess, do you think your rich-ass husband will understand? I saw how you looked at that oldest son of yours. How will he feel when he knows his mommy likes to fuck around? Do you tell every man you meet that you haven't had sex with your husband since before the birth of your last child? Do you always give men blowjobs in public restrooms? Do you kiss strangers the first time you meet them? How many people know about that sexy little heart-shaped mole of yours?"

Vera said nothing but just stared at Anthony. She was dressed and ready to go.

"Now come over here and give me a kiss goodbye, princess."

Obediently, she walked to the bed. Anthony reached out, grabbed her by the arm, and jerked her atop him. Violently, he kissed her, bruising her lips.

"Be here at noon tomorrow. I keep what's mine," he whispered into her mouth.

For the rest of the week, Vera drifted through a sexual fog. No longer protesting, she submissively showed up at his motel room each day at whatever time he dictated. Sometimes his lovemaking was generous and he kept her on the edge, making her weep and beg for completion. Other times, it was rough and demanding, as if her body was no more than a receptacle for his lust.

His sexual proclivities were dark and varied. By the end of the week, he had used her in ways she had never imagined—or desired. In spite of the humiliation and the pain, she returned. In some peculiar way, she craved what he gave her and found it impossible to resist.

On Friday afternoon, the day before the Coulson Halloween party, Vera was again in the motel room with

Anthony. He seemed to be in a generous mood and lulled her into a sense of security as he brought her to a violent climax. Sleepily enjoying the pleasurable aftermath, Vera was jolted back to reality when she found Anthony's hands wrapped around her throat as he squeezed tightly, as if trying to drain the life from her body.

Gasping for air, her eyes bulging, she frantically grabbed his wrists, trying to pull them away. Just when she thought she would pass out, he released her. Coughing violently and trying to catch her breath, Vera grabbed her throat and rubbed the injured area. Looking wildly at Anthony, she was confused.

Coolly, Anthony grabbed hold of her chin and forced her to look him in the eyes.

"I just want you to understand—I mean really understand—I own you now. I have the power to end your life with very little effort."

"I don't understand," she gasped, terrified for her life.

"I love you, Vera. I've never felt this way about a woman before. But if I ever find out you've fucked your husband again—or any man but me—I will kill you and him. I won't even think twice. Do you understand?"

With tear-filled eyes, Vera nodded.

Whatever demons possessed Anthony, they vanished as quickly as they had appeared.

"Don't be afraid, baby," Anthony whispered into her ear. He then moved on top of Vera, kissing her, stroking her body reverently. "I love you so much, baby, I can't help myself."

"Please don't be mad at me," Vera cried out, wrapping her arms around Anthony, holding him tight. "I'll do whatever you want, I promise. I'm yours, Anthony, no one else's."

Wanting Vera to prove her devotion, Anthony took her

in the roughest way he knew how—in the way she found most painful, humiliating, and unnatural. Without complaint, she took it all, each painful thrust he inflicted.

VERA HAD MENTIONED THE SATURDAY HALLOWEEN PARTY TO Anthony, telling him it would be impossible for her to get away. He seemed to understand and told her not to worry. They could see each other on Sunday, after church.

On Saturday morning, Vera started her period and felt a tremendous sense of relief. She was not pregnant. Trying to put Anthony out of her mind, she directed the household staff in preparing the final touches for her party.

That evening, party guests arrived in costume, many wearing masks in a spirited attempt to conceal their identity. Never once did she imagine Anthony would be so bold as to crash her party, especially considering he didn't seem that interested in knowing about the event.

He came as a pirate, and even she did not recognize his true identity at first. It wasn't until he asked her to dance and whispered into her ear did she know who it was. She was both frightened and titillated to know her secret lover had found his way into her party and her arms.

"Come upstairs with me to some hidden room, and fuck me. It's been too long."

"It was only yesterday," she said, careful to keep her voice down. "Unfortunately, that time of month came this morning, so I'm afraid it will be a week before we can be together again."

"Meet me upstairs—in a room of your choosing."

"Don't you understand, I said—"

"Oh, I understand. I want you on your knees. I've always been fond of you in that position. What room, princess?"

"Go up to the third floor...I'll go first. The first room on the left. The rooms on the third floor are never used. You can use the back staircase. No one will see you. Down the hall, past the library. I'll go up the main staircase. If anyone sees me, they'll assume I'm just going to freshen up."

ALONE ON THE THIRD FLOOR OF COULSON HOUSE, VERA Coulson submissively went to her knees and followed the instructions of her demanding lover.

When he was finished with her, he zipped up his pants and watched as she awkwardly got to her feet. "You're getting very good at that."

"Let me leave first," she suggested.

"First I need to tell you something. I got a phone call today. I need to go out of town for the week on business. I'll be back late Friday night. Come over Saturday at noon. Plan to stay longer than normal. I have a feeling that after a week without you, it'll take me all afternoon to get my fill."

CHAPTER THIRTEEN

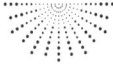

*L*ooking in the mirror, Randall straightened his tie. Glancing briefly at the reflection of the younger man lounging on the bed behind him, he gave his tie a final wiggle before he was satisfied with its appearance. He turned around.

"John, I have a favor to ask you," Randall asked.

"Certainly, you name it." John Weber lit a cigarette and took a drag. He set the cigarette in the ashtray on the table next to the bed.

"There's someone I'd like you to check out." Randall walked toward the bed and sat down on a chair. He faced John.

"Anyone I know?"

"I don't think so. His name is Anthony Marino. He's staying at Cliffwood Motel."

"What does he look like?" John asked. He reached for his cigarette and took another drag.

"Italian, looks like he should be a Vegas entertainer."

"Sounds hot."

Randall chuckled. "The man has raw sexuality, but I

have a feeling his interests lie elsewhere. In fact, I am certain of it. It's my daughter-in-law."

"Vera screwing around on Harrison? I find that hard to believe. I've never heard a whisper of her stepping out."

"I don't believe she ever has—until now. While I'm not in the habit of monitoring my children's sex life, I'm concerned she may be in over her head. Something about the man, I think he may be dangerous."

"Have you spoken to Harrison about it?"

"No. I'd rather just handle it."

"Like you do with everything." John flashed him a smile. He stood up and walked toward the chair. Bending down, John brushed his lips over Randall's.

"So will you do it?" Randall asked when the brief kiss ended.

"Have I ever denied you anything? I'll see what I can find out."

"When?"

John laughed. "I'll get right on it. Promise." He glanced at his wristwatch. "But I have to go, or I'll be late for the meeting. I'll call you later."

Before leaving, John lifted the foot of the mattress off the floor until the Murphy bed disappeared into the wall of Randall's office. Giving Randall a final wink, John strolled from the room while straightening his own tie.

———

THE DOOR TO RANDALL COULSON'S PRIVATE OFFICE OPENED and Maryanne Peterson looked up from her desk. John Weber walked out, straightening his tie. Maryanne smiled. *He is so handsome,* she thought. Of course, he was too old for her. She guessed he was in his fifties. A widower, he had never remarried, and from what she understood, he had been working for Randall Coulson since the family moved to Coulson in 1949.

Maryanne had only been Randall's secretary for six months. His previous secretary had gotten married, and the groom wanted his new wife to stay at home.

"I've a call on hold for Mr. Coulson. Are you done with your meeting? Can I put the call through?"

"I believe Mr. Coulson stepped into the restroom," John told her. "Perhaps you should give him a few minutes before you put any calls through.

"Yes, sir. Thank you, Mr. Weber."

John flashed Maryanne a smile then left Randall Coulson's outer office.

LATER THAT AFTERNOON, AS MARYANNE BEGAN GETTING READY to go home for the evening, John Weber walked back into her office.

"Is he in there?" John asked.

"Yes, he just got off the phone."

"Please tell him I'm here. He asked me for some papers earlier, and I brought them."

"Would you like me to take them in for you?"

"No, thanks. I'm afraid I need to go over a few of them with him."

"Okay." Maryanne picked up her telephone to ring her boss. When he got on the phone, she explained Mr. Weber was here to see him and had brought the papers he had requested.

"He said to go right in," Maryanne said when she hung up the phone.

"So what were you able to find out?" Randall asked as he lit his cigar and leaned back in his desk chair.

John took the chair next to the desk and opened the file he had hastily prepared.

"Before checking into the Cliffwood, he was staying with his sister and brother-in-law—Nick and Gina Carracci. It looks like Carracci and his wife are straight arrows. They have a boardinghouse up at Clement Falls and a little girl. It appears Carracci is not fond of his brother-in-law, but his wife is always trying to bail out her brother.

"I don't think Vera is in imminent danger, because according to my sources, Marino left town for the week but intends to return next Saturday. I'm not really sure where he went, but his car doesn't seem to be anywhere in town. If Vera is having an affair with him, I really couldn't find anything to support that."

"So what about his past? Do I need to be concerned?" Randall asked.

"He's been married three times. The first wife died in childbirth. But the second wife, she was murdered. Strangled. I talked to some cops in Long Island, and they're certain he was involved, but he had an airtight alibi and they couldn't pin it on him. Apparently, a second body was found around the same time. The guy had been shot. According to a close friend of Marino's dead wife, the wife was having an affair with the dead guy."

"This doesn't sound promising. What about the third wife?"

"He had a son with the third wife. Apparently, he used to knock her around a lot. She got tired of being his punching bag and took off with the kid."

"Are you sure she took off? You think he killed her?" Randall asked.

"I don't think so. Her family isn't screaming for the cops to look into her disappearance. They don't seem to be talking."

"What about the rest?"

"Well, it looks like he was hanging out with some heavy hitters back east. According to a couple guys I talked to, they're convinced he's a hit man for one of the crime families back there. There's definitely some connection between him and Vincent Santiago."

"The crime boss?"

"Yes. Word has it he sent Marino out here to cool off. Not sure what happened. There aren't any warrants out on him, but the cops I talked to say he's bad news."

"Anything else, John?"

"No. That's about all I could find on such short notice."

"You did great. You always do." Randall leaned over and patted John's knee.

"So what are you going to do with the information?"

"I haven't decided. But it looks like I may have a little time to think about it if he is out of town. Maybe we'll be lucky and he won't return."

"I hope so. By the way, I'm having a poker game tomorrow night, you want to come over?" John asked.

"Who'll be there?"

"Just me."

"I'll be there." Randall smiled. "Thanks again, John, I owe you."

"Don't worry, Randall; I'll make you pay up tomorrow night." Both men laughed.

CHAPTER FOURTEEN

The week seemed to drag for Vera. Halloween was over for her on Saturday, in spite of the fact the holiday fell on Monday. She had other things on her mind. Garret went out with friends on Halloween night, and Russell met up with Tommy and Ryan to go trick-or-treating. Vera paid little attention to Russell or his Halloween costume and left it to Garret to lecture his younger brother on safety issues.

She said goodbye to her eldest son, Sonny, who flew to New York on Wednesday for the first leg of his European tour, carefully planned out by his grandfather.

Ever present on her mind was Anthony Marino. Harrison attributed Vera's gloomy mood to the fact their eldest son was leaving for six months. Vera hadn't expected to miss Anthony, but she did. Every day she drove downtown and cruised by the motel, checking to see if he might have returned early. She didn't understand the hold he had on her, but she could not deny it existed.

The morning after Sonny left for New York, Vera sat at her dressing table, looking into its mirror. Combing her hair, she thought of Anthony. Setting the brush on the marble table, she touched the side of her neck and tilted her head to the opposite side so she could get a better view. Anthony had frightened her when he had wrapped his hands around her throat and choked her, but he'd explained why he had done it. *He loves me*, she thought. She understood that kind of love. Vera had felt it from her first lover. Harrison didn't love her. He hadn't even flinched when she had ordered him out of her bed. She could not imagine issuing such a decree to Anthony. If she dared try, he would hold her down and use his body to punish her.

Vera closed her eyes and thought of her first lover. In some ways, he reminded her of Anthony—and in some ways they were nothing alike.

Chicago, 1932

VERA HAD JUST CELEBRATED HER FOURTEENTH BIRTHDAY WHEN her parents left her with the Andersons for two years. Her father had accepted a diplomatic post overseas, and her mother did not want to subject her daughter to foreigners— although she herself was joining her husband on his new adventure.

Mrs. Anderson was a close friend of Vera's mother, and while the woman was rarely home, due to her numerous charity activities, Vera's parents were confident their daughter would be properly cared for while under the Andersons' roof.

Vera didn't object to the arrangement as she had a schoolgirl crush on the handsome Mr. Anderson. He looked like a movie star and never treated Vera like a child. He made her feel grown up.

She had only been at his home for two days when he had called her into his study for a little chat. Mrs. Anderson was not at home—she rarely was—but Mr. Anderson, who had family money and didn't go to an office like her own father, seemed to spend most of his time at his estate.

"Please take a seat, Vera. You look lovely today, by the way," he greeted her when she walked into his study. "And please, shut the door behind you."

Shy and a little nervous, Vera thanked him for the compliment, shut the door, and took a seat near his desk.

"With your parents out of the country and you living in my home, I take my responsibility toward you very seriously."

"I promise I won't be any trouble," she vowed.

He chuckled at her promise and flashed a smile. "No, dear, I don't imagine you will be any trouble. My main concern is keeping you safe. Protecting you from those who might wish to do harm to such a lovely young woman."

Vera loved how he called her a young woman and not a girl. It made her feel very grown up.

"I have a little something I would like you to read. I would prefer you keep this between you and me and not say anything to my wife, to any of your friends or the staff."

"I don't understand?" Vera frowned, clearly confused.

"My dear wife sees you as a child, Vera. She refuses to acknowledge you are no longer a little girl but a budding young woman. Therefore, she would think my lessons for you unnecessary. But you are not a child, are you?"

"No, sir." Vera looked adoringly up into Fred Anderson's eyes.

He handed her an old book, its pages and cover worn and tattered.

"*The Life and Adventures of Miss Fanny Hill*," she read the title aloud.

"It's about a girl just your age. Like you, she is without her parents, and like you, she is not a child. I have a feeling you'll be able to relate to Fanny and all her adventures. Please read it, and later we can discuss the book."

"I will. And I promise I won't tell."

What she didn't know, *The Life and Adventures of Miss Fanny Hill* was considered erotica by some, yet pornographic by most. She would not find the banned book in any bookstore she might frequent.

A few days later Fred called Vera back into his study and told her to bring the book with her. She did as she was told. When they were alone in the room, he began to ask her questions about the story.

"Perhaps my mother is right, and I am just a child. I really don't understand the book," Vera confessed.

Fred smiled and then patiently began to explain the story. He reread some of the more sexually provocative passages to her.

"So you see, Vera," he said when he finally closed the book. "Evil people will conspire to steal a young girl's virtue. It's valuable. Sometimes it's best to simply rid yourself of what they want so they'll leave you alone."

"That man...the one who they sold her to, he reminds me of my music teacher."

"Yes, and I imagine your music teacher has been looking at you the same way as the man in the story looked at Fanny. But it's not really his fault. He's a man, Vera. Men are weak and it is up to you, as a woman, to always be in control of the situation. Someday, if your music teacher gets the opportunity, I don't doubt he will try to force himself on you if he believes you are still an innocent. He will use you in the same way the men used Fanny in the book."

"No," Vera said, frantically shaking her head in denial.

"Please, Vera, you are not a child, remember. I suppose if your parents were here, one of them would be discussing this with you. But since they aren't, it's up to me to do the right thing."

"I won't take music lessons anymore!"

He laughed sardonically, then shook his head at her foolishness. "If it's not him, it will be someone else. It's your innocence they want—your first time. Just as with Fanny. Remember the story. Men can sense a young girl's innocence. Once it is gone, you won't be as vulnerable."

"I don't understand. What should I do?"

"Well," Fred began, studying Vera's expression, "if you were my daughter, I would urge you to find an older man—someone you trusted—someone you found attractive—and ask him to guide you into womanhood.

"Think of it this way, Vera. Imagine you're given a gold ring with a very large diamond. When you're out, alone, without protection, thieves will see the diamond and want it. Once you lose the diamond, you can wear the gold ring without as much fear. Oh, I'm not saying thieves won't still want your gold ring, but you'll be much safer than you were when it had a diamond.

"Your innocence—the fact that you have never been with a man—is like a diamond that men want to steal. Give it away to the man of your choosing, and you will be safer. But do it quickly, because you're far too lovely for men to resist.

"I'm afraid a young innocent is always vulnerable to evil. I wish, for your sake, your mother would have realized—

before she left—that you are no longer a child. You need a protector. You need someone like Fanny's Charles."

It was several days before Fred showed Vera what he meant. Unfortunately, he did not gently guide her into womanhood. By the time he'd removed her clothes, she began having second thoughts. When he removed his, she knew it was not something she wanted to do. Lost in his sexual fervor, Fred held her down as he forced his way into her untried body, ignoring her cries.

When it was over, he sobbed, telling her how much he loved her, begging her to forgive him. He reminded her she had to assume some of the responsibility for his actions, as she was simply too tempting, too beautiful. Frightened and confused, she forgave him.

The next night when he slipped into her bed, she was already sleeping, therefore unprepared for the weight of his body that held her down, or the hand placed over her mouth to silence her cries.

"I am your Charles," he whispered. "I must protect you, but to do that you must submit to me like Fanny submitted to Charles. Love me, Vera. Love me, Fanny." Moving his hand from her mouth, his lips covered hers. He ignored her silent protest.

In Vera's own way, she came to love Fred. She had always found him handsome, and once the initial pain subsided, he introduced her to exquisite physical pleasure. Within two months, she welcomed him into her bed, eager for his lessons. She was his Fanny—he was her Charles.

Mrs. Anderson had a fairly good idea what was going on under her roof. She wasn't concerned Fred would get Vera pregnant, as he was sterile due to a childhood illness. She was actually relieved he was leaving her alone. Mrs. Anderson would let her husband have his young lover, yet when Vera's parents returned, she would have to do something to end the affair. It would be quite scandalous if Vera's parents discovered her husband had seduced their daughter.

The affair ended when Vera was seventeen. Much to Mrs. Anderson's annoyance, it was not as easy to terminate the relationship as she initially thought. It continued even after Vera's parents returned to the country and Vera moved back home.

Frustrated over her inability to break up the sordid affair, she told her husband a lie about Vera. She insisted Vera was seeing a young man, and there was talk of a marriage. Of course, it was all a lie and he would find out the truth, but she just wanted to inflict some pain, if even temporarily.

What she hadn't planned on was her husband's despair at the news. She found him the next morning, hanging in his study. He had committed suicide.

At the funeral, she found young Vera silently mourning Fred's death.

"It's your fault," Mrs. Anderson whispered to the young woman.

"I don't understand?" Vera had no idea Mrs. Anderson was aware of the affair.

"I told him you were getting married—and he killed himself. You are an evil girl, Vera. I don't know what you did to my poor husband, but you drove him to his grave."

CHAPTER FIFTEEN

*B*y the Friday after Halloween, her period had ended. However, for as much as she wanted to be with Anthony again, she did not want to get pregnant. She could not even imagine what she would do if such a thing happened. Harrison would know it wasn't his, and if Anthony demanded she get a divorce, she would be ruined. Women in her position did not get divorced and then marry their Italian lovers. What would her parents say? She came up with a plan.

On Saturday morning, Vera slipped into Garret's bedroom. It was no secret her middle son had condoms in his bathroom. She had heard Harrison and Randall joke about it. She would take a couple and then ask Anthony to start buying them. She couldn't make the purchase, and Garret would start noticing if too many were missing.

ANTHONY HAD NO IDEA HE WOULD BE SO HAPPY TO GET BACK to this shit town, but all he could think about was Vera

Coulson and what he wanted to do to her body. Ironically, he intended to be her drug, but she had become his.

She was perfection. Before his last wife got pregnant and fat, he'd used her body in unconventional ways, but she usually ended up crying while begging him to stop. He knew Vera didn't enjoy certain things he did to her—but her tears were silent and she never asked him to stop. Even when he intentionally made it more painful, she accepted the fact he owned her completely. *Perfection.*

Lounging nude on the bed, he waited for his lover to arrive. He didn't have long to wait. Five minutes early, Vera rushed into the room and into his arms. Impatient hands tugged at her clothes, desperate to get her in the same state of undress as his body.

"Wait," Vera breathlessly pleaded, gently pushing him away.

"What for?" He bit her neck and continued to grope at her clothes.

Vera handed a small package to Anthony. He didn't take it. Instead, he looked at it, perplexed, as if he didn't quite understand what she was offering him. He frowned. It was a condom.

Snatching it from her hand, he waved it in the air. "What is this for?"

"I stole it from my son's room. I thought we could use it today, and then you could buy some for later. I have a couple more in my purse. So I don't get pregnant."

Anthony froze. He stared at the small package then looked into Vera's face. The condom slipped from his hand and fell to the floor. Before she knew what happened, Anthony pulled back his hand and slapped her across the face, sending her falling to the floor.

She looked up at him, bewildered and confused, clutching her face. The sting still throbbed.

"What the fuck, you too good for my kid?" he shouted, and then kicked Vera in the belly with full force. Vera rolled into a protective ball as Anthony continued to kick her, his bare foot doing less damage than had he been wearing shoes, yet still painful.

"You think you can tell me what I can do with your body? I own you, bitch."

Reaching down, he grabbed her by the hair and pulled her to her feet. Tossing her on the bed, he punched her belly and thighs repeatedly, ignoring her pleas. When he was tired of using her like a punching bag, he slapped her face repeatedly.

"You want to see what I think about your idea of using a condom?" he shouted as he rolled her over on her belly and jerked up her skirt and ripped off her panties. Brutally, he raped her, leaving no orifice unscathed.

When his rage subsided, he let her rest before cleaning her up. The only real damage to her clothes was her underpants. Making her stand before him, he straightened her clothes and combed her hair. Still in shock, Vera could barely move.

"Pull yourself together, baby, no real damage," Anthony insisted. He had her sit on a chair and then forced her to drink a little gin. With great effort, Vera regained some of her equilibrium.

"It's your own fault, princess. You should never have brought those condoms. You know I don't like being told what to do."

Vera sat quietly on the chair and watched Anthony as he paced the room.

"Don't ever mention condoms again, you hear? You just

need to do what I say and everything will be good and go back to how it was."

Vera continued to stare.

"Damn, princess, why did you have to go and do that?" Anthony's anger resurfaced. Vera winced; she was afraid he was going to start hitting her again.

"I was really looking forward to seeing you today and you ruined it!" he shouted. Taking a deep breath, he looked down at Vera and put a finger under her chin, tilting her face upward in his direction.

"Tell me it's okay. Tell me you'll be here tomorrow," Anthony asked in a whisper. He sounded almost desperate.

"Yes. I'll be here. I promise." Vera was too terrified to say anything else. She just wanted to get out of the motel room.

"Do you still love me, baby?"

"Yes, Anthony. You know I do."

"And if I knock you up, you'll have my baby?"

"Yes, Anthony, of course. I love you."

"I need you to prove it to me."

"I don't understand." Vera trembled in fear.

"Get on your knees, baby. Do your best. Show me how much you need me."

Vera almost asked *now* but caught herself in time. He was on the verge of going into another fit of rage.

Feeling ill, she slid off the chair to the floor onto her knees and looked up at Anthony. He smiled down at her, pleased that even with her bruised face and eyes brimming with tears, she was prepared to do whatever he demanded. *Perfection*.

CHAPTER SIXTEEN

*H*arrison wondered where everyone was when he returned home late Saturday afternoon, after a game of golf. According to one member of the household staff, his wife had gone shopping; Garret was up at Clement Falls with friends; Russell was at the park, playing baseball; and his father was at the office.

After making himself a ham sandwich in the kitchen, he headed upstairs to take a shower. When he reached the second floor, he paused a moment and rubbed his left leg. It ached. The leg had been shot up during the war, and while he still had a slight limp, it rarely gave him problems. He suspected the pain was due to the fact he chose to walk the golf course that day instead of using a cart.

Giving the leg a final rub, he straightened his posture and continued on his way. Turning down the hallway leading to his room, he noticed Vera down the corridor, rushing to her bedroom. She had obviously entered the house by the rear staircase, and she didn't see Harrison.

The way Vera dashed down the hallway, as if the devil were on her tail, seemed peculiar to Harrison. Vera never ran anywhere. Picking up his step, Harrison went to Vera's room instead of his own, finishing the last bites of his sandwich on the way.

When he walked into her room, he noticed her clothes strewn along the floor, leading a path to her bathroom, as if she couldn't get undressed fast enough. Approaching her bathroom, he heard the shower running and then something else—sobs—hysterical and uncontrollable sobs.

Silently, Harrison entered the bathroom; the door was ajar. The first thing he noticed, she hadn't even bothered to shut the shower door in spite of the fact she stood under the showerhead, its water beating down on her nude body while the overspray drenched the bath mat on the floor.

It had been years since he had seen Vera's nude body. After Russell's birth, she had made it clear he was no longer welcome in her bedchamber, and being a man of pride, he refused to beg favors from his wife. There were plenty of women cheerfully willing to give him what his wife refused.

Vera did not realize she wasn't alone. Harrison watched in fascination as she frantically scrubbed her body with a bar of soap, trying desperately to remove something from her skin. What it was, Harrison had no idea.

Harrison stepped closer; then he saw it. Her body was covered with angry bruises. Someone had severely beaten his wife. Fury swelled in Harrison, and he lurched toward the shower, turning off the water with a violent jerk. Still sobbing, Vera turned to face the intruder. Both her expression and reaction indicated she was in some state of confusion.

When Vera saw who it was, she did the last thing he expected. Instead of getting angry at Harrison for invading her privacy, Vera threw her nude, wet body into his arms, clinging onto her husband in a fit of desperation. The sobs

intensified, and the pair crumpled to the bathroom floor—
Harrison holding onto Vera as she clung to him.

It seemed like an eternity to Harrison, waiting for Vera
to regain some modicum of composure so she might explain
what had happened. Patiently, he stroked her hair and
promised that whatever it was, he would help her.
Awkwardly, he reached toward the shower door as he
continued to hold Vera and grabbed a dry towel from the
bar to wrap over her body. It was getting chilly in the bathroom and she was both wet and nude.

When she was finally ready to talk, she told him everything. Vera did not leave out a single detail, nor did she
make excuses for her behavior. Harrison sat quietly on the
bathroom floor, holding his wife, listening to her painful
confession.

Harrison was beginning to get a cramp in his bad leg
because of the awkward position, but it seemed inconsequential to what his wife had just told him. Very gently, he
eased Vera to her feet, explaining to her, in the kindest voice
possible, that she needed to rinse the rest of the soap from
her body.

He had her stand in the shower. Vera stood passively, her
eyes looking down, as Harrison tenderly rinsed away the
soap residue. After turning off the water, he guided her from
the shower, dried her body with a towel, and led her into the
bedroom.

Like a child, Vera let Harrison tuck her into bed.
Harrison sat on the side of the bed, looking down at Vera,
who stared up at him with vacant eyes. Tenderly, Harrison
brushed the damp hair from her eyes.

"I think I need to call the doctor," Harrison told her.

"No!" She began to cry again.

"Shh...please don't cry, I'm here. I'll take care of everything."

"You aren't going to leave me?" Vera asked with a pitiful voice.

"No, Vera. I'm not leaving you."

"But he will kill you!" Vera sobbed.

"Let me take care of everything."

From Vera's medicine cabinet Harrison retrieved two sleeping pills, which he insisted she take with a glass of water. He sat by her side until she drifted off to sleep. Picking up the phone beside her bed, he dialed his father's private office number.

"You need to come home. It's urgent," Harrison said after Randall answered the phone. His next call was to the family doctor.

While waiting for the doctor to arrive, he explained to the household staff that Vera did not wish to be disturbed. She had taken a sleeping pill and was resting after injuring her ankle in a fall.

The doctor and Randall arrived at the same time. Randall and Harrison went to the library to discuss the situation while the doctor examined Vera.

"MAY I COME IN?" DR. PHILLIPS ASKED AS HE OPENED THE door to the library. Harrison sat on the small sofa while his father sat across from him on a leather chair. Both men looked toward the doorway.

"Of course," Harrison said.

Just as the doctor entered the room, Russell rushed in, pushing past the doctor.

"They said Mom sprained her leg; can I go see her?" Russell asked.

"No, Russell, she's resting. Now you just rudely pushed by Dr. Phillips; please say you're sorry and leave so the adults can talk," Harrison told him.

"Oh, sorry, Doc. Can I stay and listen?" Russell asked.

"No, Russell, please do as I say. And shut the door," Harrison said.

Russell gave a shrug of defeat then turned and left the room, closing the door behind him. The doctor approached the two men so he could keep his voice low.

"Perhaps we might want to discuss this in private," the doctor said, looking uneasily at Randall.

"My father already knows everything. Please tell us Vera's condition."

After a brief pause the doctor said, "Your wife has been raped. There is severe vaginal and anal bruising. She tells me she just finished her period, so I doubt there's a chance of pregnancy. I'm planning to run some blood tests to rule out any other complications. There doesn't seem to be any internal damage. She tells me she doesn't know the identity of the rapist."

"No. She has no idea," Harrison said.

"Where did this happen? She wouldn't say."

"Your primary concern is the health of my daughter-in-law." Randall spoke up. "We're already working with the police chief on this, but naturally we want to keep this quiet —for Vera's sake. She's already been through so much; I don't think we want her to become the topic of local gossip. We expect your total discretion in this matter."

"Naturally," the doctor agreed.

"Thank you, Dr. Phillips." Harrison stood up and walked the doctor to the front door.

"MOTHER WENT WHERE?" GARRET ASKED THE FOLLOWING morning at the breakfast table. His father had just announced they wouldn't be going to church because his mother had gone to California.

"San Francisco. We were a little concerned with her ankle, and there's a specialist there we want her to see," Harrison explained. He glanced up at a member of the kitchen staff who had just entered the dining room, bringing a plate of biscuits and pitcher of gravy to the table. Silently, Harrison poured himself a cup of coffee.

"But she didn't say goodbye!" Russell said.

"What time did she leave?" Garret asked. It was understood, without saying, she had been transported in his grandfather's private plane.

"Around five this morning," Randall said. "We didn't imagine you'd want us to wake you at that time."

"You didn't know last night she was going? Can she even see someone today, on a Sunday?" Garret questioned.

"It was all very last minute and I don't understand why you're so curious about the details. We felt she needed to see a specialist and figured the sooner she got there, the best chances she'd have for a full recovery." Harrison sounded annoyed.

"It's just so typical of Mother," Garret said under his breath. Angrily he speared a piece of scrambled egg.

"What is that supposed to mean?" Harrison glared at his son.

"She gets all dramatic over some sprained ankle. I don't know why she refused to see Russell last night. The kid was worried about her."

"It's okay, Garret." Russell hated to hear his father and brother argue.

"No, it's not!" Garret snapped.

"Last night I gave your mother a sleeping pill. She was sleeping when Russell got home. Was it really so important for your brother to watch her sleep? Now who is acting all dramatic?"

"But to just leave this morning, not even say goodbye to Russell, when he was clearly worried?" Garret asked angrily.

"Garret, I said it was okay!" Russell tossed his fork on the table, scooted his chair back, quickly stood up, and ran from the room.

"Now who is upsetting the boy?" Randall asked.

"I just hate how Mother ignores him." Garret looked guiltily at the doorway where Russell had disappeared.

"She doesn't treat Russell any different than she treats you," Harrison defended his wife.

"No, she doesn't, Father. I'm just used to it."

Harrison stopped eating, closed his eyes for a moment, and took a deep breath. With forced calm, he addressed Garret. "I didn't want to say anything around Russell, but it looks like the fall did some serious damage to your mother's ankle. Her level of pain...well, was quite excruciating, and I really didn't think it would be wise for your brother to see her like that. I understand you have some issues with your mother. But right now, she can't deal with your issues. And frankly, neither can I." Harrison abruptly stood up, tossed his linen napkin on the table, and left the room without finishing his breakfast.

CHAPTER SEVENTEEN

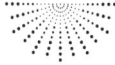

"*I* don't like the idea of the Pope telling us what to do," Charley Jones grumbled. He sat with Wally Keller in the Cliffwood Motel's front office, drinking his second cup of coffee. "I'm a Baptist, damnit."

Wally chuckled. "I don't think the Pope is going to tell us what to do."

"Kennedy is a damn Catholic. And I know how it works. Those Catholics do what their Pope says, and before you know it, some foreign Pope is going to be running this country!" It had been a week since the presidential election, and Jones hadn't gotten over the fact Kennedy had won.

"I've got other things on my mind than to worry about the Pope," Wally told Charley.

"What's going on?" Charley had moved to Coulson five years earlier, after retiring. He spent his mornings visiting the various shop owners along Main Street, and he had struck up a friendship with Wally when the Kellers first took over the motel.

"Remember that tenant I told you about, in room ten?" Wally asked.

"The fancy dresser, with the Lincoln Continental?"

"That's him. I think he left."

"I thought he was staying for the month."

"That's what he said."

"If he left without paying, I'd call the cops on him."

"No, that's not it. He came in the office the end of the month, the Saturday before Halloween, and paid for November. Told me he'd be gone for a week, but he wanted to keep the room, so he paid for another month."

"Maybe something came up on his trip, delayed his return," Charley suggested.

"No, he did return the next Saturday. I saw him in the morning, asked him how his trip went. He said everything went fine but that he was glad to be back. In fact, he told me he wouldn't be going anywhere for the rest of November."

"What does this guy do again?"

"I don't know; he was checking into some local businesses, something like that. I got the impression he was an investor or looking for a business to buy. But the thing is, Charley, the next morning, on Sunday, his car was gone. I didn't think anything about it at the time. But he hasn't been back. That was over a week ago."

"Have you checked his room?"

"No. I feel sort of funny barging in there. It has the do-not-disturb hanger on the door."

"Does he have any friends you could ask? Did he leave some contact number?"

"He mentioned something about a sister up in Clement Falls. But I never saw him with anyone. No one ever visited him at the motel."

"I'd go check out his room. Who knows, might be a dead body in there!" Charley said excitedly.

"I doubt that, his car is gone."

"Maybe someone killed him, stole his car. I think you should go check his room."

"I don't know. Maybe I should call the police."

"I tell you what, I'll go with you. Let's go check his room now. It's your motel. You have the right to go in there." Charley stood up, anxious to see the room.

Wally silently considered Charley's suggestion.

"Okay, let's do it." Wally pulled the key ring from his pocket and headed to the door. Outside, Charley followed Wally down the walkway leading to room ten. The temperature had significantly dropped in the last week, and there was a nip in the air.

"This is it," Wally said as he got to the room. Before using the key, he knocked loudly on the door.

"Mr. Marino, hello? Are you in there?" He knocked again. When there was no answer, he unlocked the door and pushed it open. The room was dark. The drawn shades blocked out the sun. Wally reached in and switched on the overhead light. A dull yellow glow illuminated the dingy room.

The two men walked in and looked around. The bed was unmade, but there was no sign of any luggage, clothes, or personal items belonging to Anthony Marino. Wally inspected the room and found the drawers and the closet empty.

"Looks like the guy moved out," Charley said. He peeked around the room, looking for some forgotten item.

"But he paid for the month. This is so strange." Wally shook his head.

"Ahh," Charley said as he leaned down and picked something up off the floor. "Apparently your missing renter did have a visitor." Charley handed Anthony an unopened condom package he'd found on the floor, partially hidden by the bedspread hanging off the unmade bed.

"Odd." Wally took the condom package. "I never saw anyone come to his room. They'd have to pass right by my office."

"Probably was at night."

"I guess you're right. Maybe I should try to get ahold of his sister."

"Do you have her name?"

"No. The only thing I know, she and her husband have a boardinghouse up at Clement Falls."

"From what I know, there's only one, owned by Nick Carracci. Good guy. I met him a few years ago when I first started going fishing up there. Some good trout up in those streams."

Wally gave the room a final inspection before he and Charley stepped back outside.

"I wonder if I should leave this do-not-disturb hanger on?" Wally asked.

"Well, the guy did pay for the room. Maybe he took a spur-of-the-moment trip to go see his sister."

"I guess I'll try giving them a call." Wally locked the door.

Before Charley left the motel, he looked up the Carracci number in the phone book.

"Let me know how this turns out," Charley told Wally as he said goodbye. "But it would've made a far better story if there had been a dead body in the room!"

"I imagine my sons would feel the same way—but I'd rather not have people dying or getting murdered at my motel." Wally laughed.

After Charley left, Wally sat at his desk and dialed the

Carraccis' phone number. It rang and rang, and Wally was about to hang up when a man answered.

"Clement Falls Boardinghouse." There was a faint Italian accent.

"Is this Mr. Carracci?"

"Yes, how can I help you?"

"I'm calling about Anthony Marino."

Silence.

"Hello, Mr. Carracci, are you still there?"

"Yes."

"Did you hear what I said?"

"I know nothing about Anthony Marino. Don't call me again." The man abruptly hung up.

Wally stared dumbly at the phone.

"Wow, some people really hate wrong numbers," Wally said aloud to the empty office.

He redialed the number. Mr. Carracci answered the call, but this time his voice was less friendly.

"Mr. Carracci, please don't hang up—please hear me out!" Wally said in a rush. Not waiting for a reply, he continued. "I'm looking for a boardinghouse in Clement Falls, and I understood there was only one—yours. But apparently, there must be more. My name is Wally Keller, I own the Cliffwood Motel in Coulson. I had a guest who told me his sister and brother-in-law had a boardinghouse in Clement Falls, and I assumed it was yours. I'm sorry to be bothering you, but I wonder, can you direct me to any other boardinghouses up there?"

"Why do you need to contact these people?" Mr. Carracci asked.

"Mr. Marino seems to be missing. He paid for the month of November, and he told me he wasn't going anywhere. But he hasn't been here for a week, and I just wondered if perhaps he was at his sister's or if she might know where he went."

"If you're lucky, he won't come back," Mr. Carracci said in a dull tone.

"Excuse me?"

"Anthony Marino is my brother-in-law. Consider yourself lucky if he never comes back."

"I don't understand?"

"If he does come back, be careful around him. Do you understand?"

"No, Mr. Carracci, I don't understand."

"I wish I could say more, but I have a family to think about. My wife loves her brother. God knows why, but she does. I would prefer not to say or do anything that might get back to him, because he's like that bad penny; he'll be back. Just be careful, Mr. Keller, my brother-in-law is a very bad man. And please, I would appreciate it if you don't call again. I don't want to upset my wife."

After Wally hung up the phone, he considered his dilemma. Now he had an entirely different problem to consider. If Anthony Marino were really a bad man, what would Wally do if he did return? He had his sons to consider. Marino had always been friendly with the boys, but after the phone conversation with Mr. Carracci, Wally Keller was worried about his family.

Briefly, he considered calling the police station. But they would probably send over some random officer to talk to him, and Wally didn't want to waste his time. He wanted to talk directly to the police chief.

Making a decision, Wally grabbed his keys.

"SO, YOU SAY HE'S GONE?" POLICE CHIEF PETERSON ASKED. Leaning back in his swivel office chair, the overweight lawman chewed on the end of his unlit cigar as he listened to what Wally Keller had to say.

"Initially, I wondered if this was some missing-person situation, but then after I talked to his brother-in-law, I'm a little worried if he does show up. I'm not really sure what Carracci meant when he said he was a really bad man." Wally sat in the Coulson police chief's office.

"Marino is a nasty character. Been keeping an eye on him," Peterson said.

"You knew about him?"

"Of course. This is a small town, Keller. Wasn't much I could do but keep an eye on him. Man hasn't broken any laws here. No outstanding warrants. Hopefully, he won't come back and he can be someone else's problem. Now, is there anything else?"

"I don't understand. What has he done?" Keller asked, getting frustrated.

"Like I said, nothing here."

"So *why* were you keeping an eye on him?"

"Ah...that...organized crime from back east. Possible contract killer. But only rumors."

"And you didn't think it prudent to tell me? Let me know what my newest renter might be involved in?" Wally fought to keep his composure. He desperately wanted to hit the lackadaisical lawman over the head.

"I can't be spreading unfounded rumors, Keller. Like I said, I was keeping an eye on him. But seems he's moved on so not your problem anymore."

"And what do I do if he shows up again?" Keller asked.

"I suppose you have the right to deny him service. Of

course, if he already paid for the room, you might have a problem there."

Frustrated, Wally stood up abruptly and stormed out of the police chief's office. Peterson watched the angry innkeeper depart. After a moment, Peterson removed the unlit cigar from his mouth and tossed it on his desk. He picked up his phone and dialed a number. A moment later, the party he was calling answered the phone.

"Keller was just here. Apparently, he just noticed his tenant is missing."

CHAPTER EIGHTEEN

"*D*ad, when is Mr. Marino coming back?" Jimmy asked his father. "I thought you said he was staying for November." Jimmy missed the candy bars the man had left in the mailbox each morning.

"I don't think he is coming back," Wally told his son. Muttering to himself, he added, "I sure as hell hope not."

"Can we order pizza tonight?" Ryan asked as he dipped his cookie in a glass of cold milk. He and his brother had just gotten home from school and were having their afternoon snack. Wally stood in the kitchen, washing the dishes left over from breakfast.

"I suppose, it is Friday night," Wally said.

Abruptly, Jimmy dropped his cookie, rushed to the window, and looked out. "Hey, Dad, a cop car just pulled up in front of the motel, and they're getting out! Oh, there's another car behind them, men in suits!"

Wally dropped the dishtowel on the counter and looked out the window.

"That's a sheriff's car, not the local police," Wally said.

"What's the difference?" Jimmy asked.

Ryan shoved the second cookie in his mouth and rushed to the window to see. Four men walked toward the office door, two wore uniforms. Wally Keller moved from his kitchen to the office just as the office door opened and the men entered.

"Can I help you?" Wally greeted the men, curious to see what was going on.

"I'm Agent Carmichael and this is Agent Stephens." He showed Wally his identification. They were from the FBI.

"We're looking for this man," Stephens said. He handed Wally a black-and-white photograph. It was a picture of Anthony Marino.

"That's Mr. Marino. He rented a room here," Wally told them.

Ryan and Jimmy quietly listened from behind the counter. Standing on tiptoes, they tried to see what was going on, but their father waved them back, silently telling the boys that he did not want them in the office.

"Is he here now?" Stephens asked.

"No, he hasn't been here, well, for close to two weeks now," Wally told them.

"When was the last time you saw him?"

"Let's see...when he got back the first time." Wally glanced at his calendar. "That would have been Saturday morning, November fifth."

"You say he had just got back, when did he leave?" Carmichael asked.

"He came in here the Saturday before Halloween. Told me he was leaving for a week and paid November's rent. Not sure when he left exactly, but I didn't see his car on Sunday. He showed up again the next Saturday, said he wasn't planning to go anywhere. That was the last time I saw him."

"Do you have any idea where he may have gone?" Stephens asked.

"No. I already spoke to Police Chief Peterson about this," Keller told them.

"Really?" Stephens said as he glanced to his partner.

"I was concerned my renter was missing. And then I spoke to his brother-in-law." Wally paused and then looked down at his sons, who were still listening behind the counter.

"Boys," Wally said to his sons, "I would like you to go to your bedroom so I can talk privately with these gentlemen."

"Ah, gee, Dad," both boys whined in unison. Wally gave them a stern look. They did as they were told.

"We would like to talk to the boys later," Agent Carmichael told him.

"I suppose that would be okay, but I really didn't want them to hear what I was about to say. I spoke to Mr. Marino's brother-in-law, and from what he said, I got the impression Marino wasn't the type of man I wanted around my boys. So I went to have a talk with the police chief. He said they knew about Marino's reputation, and they were keeping an eye on him."

"Right now we're more interested in Marino's whereabouts during the first week of November," Agent Carmichael said.

"I'm afraid I can't help you there. He never said anything about where he was going, just that it was for business."

"Have you cleaned his room?" Agent Carmichael asked.

"No. But I did go in to check things. He's paid through November, so I felt funny doing anything with the room until the end of the month."

"We'd like to see it," Stephens said.

"Certainly." Wally took out his keys.

WALLY WAITED OUTSIDE ROOM TEN WHILE THE OFFICERS looked through the room. When they finally came back outside, the questions resumed.

"Did Marino ever bring anyone to his room? Did you see him with anyone?" Stephens asked.

"No. Never. But I think he may have brought a woman to the room."

"Why do you say that?"

"When I looked at the room the other day, I found an unopened condom package on the floor by the bed. I know that wasn't there when he rented the room."

"Can I see it?" Stephens asked.

"I...I'm afraid I threw it away," Wally confessed. They looked annoyed.

"There wasn't any trash in the can; did you dump the trash too?" one of the uniformed officers asked.

"No, I didn't touch the trash. That's right; there wasn't any trash in the can when I looked the other day. I didn't give it much thought at the time."

"I'd like to speak to the boys now," Carmichael told him.

"BOYS, THIS IS AGENT CARMICHAEL. HE HAS A FEW questions for you. I want you to tell him everything you know about Mr. Marino and answer his questions truthfully."

Agent Carmichael sat at the kitchen table while the rest of his entourage waited outside. Wearing a dark suit, Carmichael was a clean-shaven man in his early thirties, with shortly cropped dark hair.

"Are you a real G-man?" Ryan asked in awe after his father left the room.

Carmichael chuckled. "I suppose so. Now...you're Ryan... and you're Jimmy?"

Both boys nodded the affirmative.

"Okay, Jimmy first. Why don't you tell me everything you know about Mr. Marino?"

Jimmy looked nervously in the direction his father had gone. "Will you tell my dad?"

"Your dad? Is there something that happened with Mr. Marino that you don't want your dad to know?"

Jimmy nodded.

"Why don't you just tell me, Jimmy, I'm certain we can work things out."

"Well," Jimmy said as he shuffled his feet guiltily, "Mr. Marino gave us candy. He told us if we stayed away from his door and never bothered him, he would leave us candy each morning in the mailbox. And he did. Until, well, until he went away."

"And did you boys stay away from his room? Did you ever get tempted and peek? Maybe saw something you never told anyone?"

"No way!" Jimmy exclaimed. "It was really cool getting candy. I didn't want to mess things up."

Carmichael turned to Ryan. "What about you? What do you remember about him?"

"Pretty much what Jimmy said. It was cool to get the candy, and I think Dad would be pretty mad at us if he found out. But Mr. Marino was always nice to us. He'd ask us if we had fun playing ball, stuff like that."

"Did you ever see him with anyone?"

"No. Only saw him around here. Never saw him talking with anyone," Ryan said.

"Okay, boys. I appreciate you talking to me. But in the future, it's not a good idea to keep secrets from your father. If you see Mr. Marino again, tell your father immediately. I'm not going to say anything to your dad about the candy, but I wish you would."

"He was a real G-man!" Ryan told Tommy that evening on the telephone.

"So what did they want Mr. Marino for? Did he rob a bank or something?" Tommy asked.

"Must have, but they didn't say. We had to tell Dad about the candy."

"Did Jimmy rat you out?" Tommy asked.

"Dad told us we had to tell the G-man everything. And it's hard to keep something from a G-man when you're six. So I'm not really mad at Jimmy. Doesn't matter anyway, Mr. Marino left, so there's no more candy."

"So the G-man told your dad?"

"No, but he told us we should. Before I could stop Jimmy, he spilled the beans when we were eating pizza."

"So are you grounded?" Tommy asked.

"That might have been better. Dad got really upset about the candy. Then he started giving us this big old lecture about how he has to be mom and dad to us and how he wants to keep us safe. For a minute there, I thought he was going to cry. I tell you what, I wish he would have just smacked us for the candy instead of giving us that big ol' lecture."

"Hey, did you tell the G-Man about the note Mr. Marino gave Russell?"

"What note?"

"Oh, that's right. I forgot you weren't there. One day when Russell and me were on our way home, Mr. Marino asked Russell if he would give Mrs. Coulson a note for him. Said he knew Russell's parents."

"I forgot Mr. Marino told Russell he knew his parents. But I didn't know about a note."

"He gave a note to Russell for Mrs. Coulson. Something about a surprise for Russell's dad," Tommy explained.

"Did Russell give it to her?"

"I guess. I asked him later what was in the note, but he said he didn't know. Said it was some surprise for his dad, and he had to keep it a secret."

"Do you think the G-Man would want to know about the note?"

"I don't know. Do you think it would get Russell's parents in trouble?"

"They're big shots, so I don't think they could get in trouble."

"Maybe you should ask your dad," Tommy suggested.

"Yeah, I probably should. Maybe if I do, he won't be as mad about the candy."

CHAPTER NINETEEN

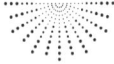

"*E*xcuse me, Mr. Harrison. There are two gentlemen here to see you." Gladys, the head of the household staff, stood at the door to the library, looking in. Harrison glanced up from the couch, where he was reading the morning paper. Randall sat at the desk in the library, going through papers.

"Who is it, Gladys?" Harrison asked.

"They say they're from the FBI."

"Did they show you some identification?" Harrison asked.

"Yes. But I don't know if it's real."

"Where are they?" Randall asked.

"Waiting on the front porch."

Randall smiled, finding it amusing that Gladys would not let them in the house.

"Show them in. We'll meet with them in the library," Harrison told her. When she left the room, he folded the newspaper and set it on his lap. He looked over to his father.

"What do you suppose this is about?" Harrison asked.

"I guess we'll have to wait and see."

A few minutes later, Gladys showed the two men into the library. Both Randall and Harrison stood up.

"I'm Agent Carmichael, and this is Agent Stephens," one of the two men said before he handed Harrison identification. Harrison looked briefly at the identification and then handed it to Randall.

"I'm Harrison Coulson." Harrison extended his right hand to the man closest to him after Randall returned the identification. The men shook hands.

"This is my father, Randall Coulson."

Randall stepped forward and shook each man's hand.

"What is this about?" Randall asked.

Carmichael looked at Harrison. "We'd like to speak to your son."

"Garret?" Harrison frowned.

"No, Russell," Carmichael clarified.

"Russell? The boy is six years old. Would you please tell me what this is about?" Harrison asked.

"We're looking for this man." Carmichael pulled a small photograph out of his coat pocket and handed it to Harrison. "His name is Anthony Marino. He was staying at the Cliffwood Motel, and apparently he had a conversation with your son."

Harrison took the photo and looked at it for a moment. He said nothing but handed it to his father. Randall glanced at the photograph for a moment, then handed it back to Carmichael.

"Yes, we know who Mr. Marino is," Randall said.

"Can you tell me what your relationship was with Marino?" Stephens asked.

"I said we know who he is, young man. Not that we have a relationship with him," Randall said coolly.

Harrison stepped out of the library for a moment and called out to Gladys, who was nearby.

"Gladys, please have Russell come to the library."

"Perhaps there's someplace we could talk to your son alone?" Stephens asked.

"No," Harrison told him. "If you want to talk to him, you can do it here, in my presence. The boy is just six years old."

Stephens and Carmichael exchanged glances. A few minutes later, Russell walked into the library. He looked curiously at the two strange men but walked straight to his father. Standing by Harrison, he looked up at the men. Harrison placed his hands on Russell's shoulders.

"Russell, this is Agent Carmichael and Agent Stephens. They have a couple of questions to ask you," Harrison told his son.

Russell looked nervously at the strangers.

"Russell." Carmichael went down on a bent knee so he could be eye level to the boy. "Do you remember this man?" He showed Russell the photograph of Anthony Marino.

Russell gave a little nod.

"I understand he gave you a note—" Carmichael paused for a moment and glanced up to Harrison "—for your mother. I'd like you to tell me about that note."

Russell said nothing but looked nervously at his father.

"Russell, it's okay," Harrison told his son. "Tell Mr. Carmichael what you know."

"No. I can't. It's a secret between Mom and me."

"Where is your wife, Mr. Coulson?" Carmichael glanced up at Harrison.

"She's out of town. But I'm sure Russell can tell you what you need to know."

"But, Dad..." Russell protested.

"Russell," Harrison said sharply, "if your mother was

here, she would tell you the same thing. Tell these men what they need to know. We haven't time to play games."

Russell was quiet for a few moments before he started to talk. "Mr. Marino said he knew my parents and that my mom was trying to arrange a surprise for my dad. He said he could help. He told me to give the note to my mother, and I was not to say anything to anyone."

"Do you know what the surprise was?"

"No. Mom said I was to keep the note a secret."

"Did she say anything else?" Carmichael asked.

"No," Russell told him.

"Did Mr. Marino tell you anything else...anything that you haven't told me?"

"No." Russell glanced up at his father.

"You can go now, Russell. Run along." Harrison gave Russell a gentle nudge.

As Russell raced from the library, Harrison walked to the chair he had been sitting in earlier, then turned to face the men.

"Gentlemen, why don't we sit down so we can be more comfortable while we conclude our conversation," Harrison said.

A few moments later, Carmichael and Stephens sat side by side on the sofa while Randall and Harrison sat in the leather chairs facing them.

"I thought you said you didn't have a relationship with Marino," Stephens asked Randall after the four men sat down.

"I can explain," Harrison began. "One night, we were having dinner at the Roseville, a restaurant in town. My father, wife, and eldest son, Harrison Junior. Marino was there and sent some champagne over to our table."

"Why would he do that?" Stephens asked.

"I can only presume to insinuate himself into our company. He came over to our table. We were cordial with the man. Somehow, the conversation came up about men's jewelry—I can't recall exactly. It was all very inconsequential at the time. Apparently, Marino felt it was another opportunity to ingratiate himself with us. So he used our son to get a note to Vera, letting her know he had a connection and that if she wanted to surprise me with diamond cufflinks, he could get quality diamonds at a great price. My wife...well, despite the fact she can afford whatever she wants, loves a good deal. She told our son to keep the note secret."

"She contacted Marino?" Carmichael asked.

"No. I found the note later that same day, and when I realized it was from Marino, I told Vera I didn't trust the man. I figured if he had a deal, the diamonds were probably hot. She was horrified and tore up the note. She never contacted him."

"Do you have the note?" Stephens asked.

"Like I said, she tore it up. It was thrown away."

"When was the last time you saw Marino?" Stephens asked.

"At the restaurant when he sent over the champagne," Harrison explained. "I'm sure the staff over at the Roseville will verify my story."

"Now I would like to ask a question." Randall spoke up. "What is this really all about? You're obviously looking for Marino. Why?"

There was a long pause before Stephens answered Randall's question.

"There was a contract hit near Reno during the first week in November. Authorities in New Jersey have two cold cases—eerily similar to the Reno killing. They always believed Marino was behind the first two but couldn't prove it. We're trying to track down Marino so we can talk to him, but he and his car have disappeared. No one has seen him."

"Pretty obvious to me," Randall said. "He's on the run. Not sure why you had to bother a six-year-old."

"We're just trying to track down any lead we can find for some clue to his whereabouts."

"Well"—Harrison stood up—"we'll be happy if he doesn't return to Coulson. But if he does, we'll contact you immediately. Do you have a card?"

"WELL, THAT WAS A BIG WASTE OF TIME," STEPHENS TOLD Carmichael as the two men returned to their car.

"Did you honestly believe a note to a six-year-old might lead us to Marino?" Carmichael asked as they got into the car.

"You have to admit, it did sound intriguing. A note passed to the grande dame of Coulson." Stephens chuckled as he started the engine.

"Well, it looks as if Marino is on the run," Carmichael said.

"Funny though, not really his MO. I would've expected him to be waiting at the motel, offering us a cup of coffee while he taunts us and comes up with one of his famous alibis."

"True. But maybe he's just screwing with us."

"You think he'll return to the Cliffwood?"

"I suppose it's possible. But no one's seen his car for a couple of weeks, so I imagine he's miles from here."

CHAPTER TWENTY

*H*arrison absently gazed out the side window of the Cessna, paying little attention to the fast approach of the landing strip or the sound of the undercarriage moving into place as the plane prepared for landing. Touchdown's modest thud returned Harrison to the present and he stirred restlessly in the seat, anxious to exit the plane. Impatient for the pilot to bring the aircraft to the far end of the runway, Harrison wanted to get on with today's agenda. He was going to see Vera.

There was a car waiting for him at the end of the runway. Harrison climbed out of the plane, its propeller still spinning. Giving the prop a wide berth, he hastily made his way to the waiting vehicle, dodging the propeller's furious windstorm.

It was a short drive to the private sanitarium. They were expecting his arrival and security was efficient. Harrison didn't have to wait long. In a matter of minutes, he was inside the building and being led down the hallway to his wife's room while the attending physician told him of Vera's progress.

When Harrison had delivered Vera to the sanitarium the Sunday morning after the attack, he was relieved to find the institution not as depressing as he imagined it might be. His father had assured him it was the best place for Vera; they would give her the care she needed.

At first, she had begged him not to leave her, clinging onto his arm. He promised he would return, telling her they could provide the help she needed and that he was unable to give.

"You'll be safe here," he told her.

"And he won't find me?" she had asked, her eyes still wild and fearful.

"No, Vera, he will never find you here." His promise seemed to calm her, and while the doctor on admission still insisted a sedative be administered, she took it submissively and did not resist.

HE FOUND HER SITTING IN A CHAIR, LOOKING OUT HER window. Had it been spring, the view of the flower garden outside her room might have been a cheerful sight. But no colorful blossoms were in bloom, and it seemed a sad and dreary picture.

She wore one of the casual dresses he had hastily packed for the trip. That surprised him. He expected to find her wearing a robe or nightgown. Vera heard him enter the room and turned to face him. She wore no makeup. His wife seemed younger somehow. There was vulnerability in her expression, which hadn't been there before the attack.

"You came." Her voice was faint. She gave him a sad smile.

"I told you I would."

She didn't stand to greet him when he approached. Harrison leaned down and kissed her forehead. Glancing around, he noticed an empty chair across the room. He walked over and picked it up, then set it next to Vera. Harrison sat down. Reaching out, he took her right hand and held it.

"How are you feeling? The doctor says you're making great progress."

"I'm feeling much better. I want to thank you for bringing me here, Harrison. I'm sorry I fought you about it." She gave his hand a little squeeze and withdrew it from his hold. Folding her hands together on her lap, she looked up at her husband. "Do you hate me, Harrison?" Her eyes searched his.

"No, Vera. I don't hate you. I want you to come home. The doctor says you should be able to be home by Christmas."

"I would rather stay here. I'm content here."

"You can't stay, Vera. Your place is at home."

"He'll find me there."

"I told you, Vera, you don't have to worry about him. Ever again."

"Are you sure?"

"Yes. Positive. He won't hurt anyone ever again. But before you come home, there are some things you need to know. The FBI was looking for him."

"Why?" Vera frowned.

"They suspect he killed someone the first week in November."

"Who?"

"I don't know. It was a contract hit."

"Anything else?" She looked as if she might get ill.

"They know about the note, the one he gave to Russell. It's a good thing you told me about it."

"What do they know about me...and him?"

"Just what I told them. I mentioned meeting him at the restaurant, the champagne he sent over. I fabricated a story about a discussion over men's jewelry, saying he sent you a note, telling you he could get you a deal. I said I found the note that afternoon, and after telling you whatever he might get would probably be stolen merchandise, you tore up the note and never called him."

"Men's jewelry?" Vera smiled. "You've never worn anything but a watch."

"It was the only thing I could come up with. When they showed up and asked to speak to Russell, the whole time—while waiting for Russell to tell his version of the story—I racked my brain, trying to come up with something."

"Thank you, Harrison. But really, leave me here. It would be for the best."

"The boys miss you. You need to come home."

"Garret? I find that hard to believe."

"I suppose Garret is more angry because of Russell. He feels your hasty departure showed a lack of consideration for his younger brother. But he doesn't understand."

"Garret—we are a constant disappointment to each other."

"Russell is sad you won't be home for Thanksgiving, but I promised him you'll be back by Christmas."

"Christmas, I forgot. It's almost that time. I suppose I'll miss the annual Coulson party."

"You don't have to. All your friends have been told the story about your ankle and how you've been in private therapy. They'll be delighted to see you."

"Yes, I've received the letters and cards you forwarded. But I haven't heard from Sonny."

"Well, you know Sonny. He's never been good at letter writing. Of course, we had to tell him the ankle story in case he called the house. I haven't spoken to him, but my father talks to him once a week."

"Harrison, what happens when I return home? What happens with us?"

Studying his wife's expression, he did not answer immediately.

"We'll go back to how we were before. Before Anthony Marino came into our lives."

HARRISON RETURNED TO COULSON THAT AFTERNOON. ONLY his father and the pilot knew he had gone out of town. Before leaving the sanitarium, Harrison again discussed Vera's progress with the doctor. They agreed that if things continued to proceed as they had been, she could come home by Christmas.

THANKSGIVING DINNER AROUND THE COULSON TABLE LACKED a female presence. Randall invited John Weber to share the meal with them in Vera's absence. Bored with the company and dinner conversation, Garret made his hasty departure after dessert and took off to hook up with friends whose parents didn't insist they hang around the house Thanksgiving evening.

Russell was not so lucky. He took his slice of pumpkin pie into the living room to avoid the stinky cigar smoke clouding the dining room air. After finishing their dessert, the three men remained at the table, discussing business and politics.

Instead of turning on the television, Russell sat on the couch and silently ate his pie while thinking of his friends. Wondering what they were doing today, he couldn't help but envy them their lives.

Ryan had a kid brother to hang out with. While Russell had Garret, Garret never wanted to play army men or games. The cool thing about a kid brother, if you didn't want to hang out with him, you didn't have to. But if you wanted someone to play with, he was always willing. Jimmy was always anxious to be included in whatever Ryan wanted to do.

Russell wasn't sure he would want sisters. Tommy's sisters liked to play with silly dolls. However, he liked looking at girls. He didn't know why, but they fascinated him. He also liked Tommy's mom and dad. They were different from his parents. Sometimes Mr. Chamberlain would play ball with the boys, and Mrs. Chamberlain would talk to him like she really cared about what he had to say.

THE DAY AFTER THANKSGIVING, WALLY KELLER STOOD ON THE ladder, hanging Christmas lights on the motel while his sons watched from below, ready to hand him whatever he might need. Just as he was making his way down the ladder, a car pulled into the motel parking lot.

The car stopped and a young woman and small child got out of the vehicle. After taking the toddler's hand in hers, the woman walked toward Wally and his sons.

"Good morning," Wally greeted her. Absently, he wiped his hands on his denims.

"Hello, are you Mr. Keller?" She was a pretty thing, with large brown eyes and thick raven-colored hair cascading down her back. Curvy and round, she was about five feet two inches tall. If he was to guess, he would say she was Italian.

"Yes."

"My name is Gina Carracci. Anthony Marino is my brother."

Wally didn't respond immediately. Finally, he asked, "How can I help you?"

"My brother is missing, and I understand he was staying here."

"Yes, he was. He rented a room for November, but I haven't seen him since the first part of the month. I assume he decided to leave at the last moment. He didn't leave anything in his room."

"I've talked to the police, but they won't help me. Everyone seems to think Anthony just took off. But I know he wouldn't have left without contacting me. He's never gone a week without calling me, letting me know he's okay."

"I'm sorry, Mrs. Carracci; I don't know what to tell you."

"Can I see his room, please?"

Wally considered her request for a moment. Then he smiled and dug his keys out of his jeans pocket.

"Sure, it's this way. Boys, put the ladder and my tools away while I show Mrs. Carracci room ten."

Gina followed Wally down the walkway as he fumbled with his key ring, looking for the right key.

"I haven't touched the room," he told her. "He did pay until the end of the month. I was planning on preparing it for another renter on the first." Wally unlocked and opened the door. After flipping on the light, he stepped aside so Gina could enter.

Wally followed her into the room. She looked around, as if some secret to Marino's disappearance would be written on the walls.

"This is not like Anthony," she whispered, looking around the room. "Something is very wrong." She turned and looked at Wally.

"People do not understand my brother. They say he has done bad things. But he is my brother; I love him. When I was a child, he always took care of me."

"I wish I could help you, ma'am. If he comes back, I promise I'll call you."

"He won't come back." Her eyes filled with tears. "I can feel it. Anthony died in this room. His spirit is still here, trapped. Something evil happened here, Mr. Keller. Something very evil."

CHAPTER TWENTY-ONE

On Thursday morning, December first, Wally Keller cleaned out room ten. Alone in the motel room, the memory of Gina Carracci's ominous words sent chills up his spine. But when the task was complete and the space aired out, it seemed no different from his other motel rooms.

As the month progressed, thoughts of Anthony Marino were replaced with happier ones. Ryan and Jimmy hung their Christmas stockings over a cardboard fireplace—one purchased at the local five-and-dime and assembled by their father. Christmas lights sprouted up all through town, dotting the horizon with festive colors.

At Coulson House, Gladys contacted the interior designer Mrs. Coulson employed every year and arranged for the annual decorating of the estate. It would be decked out for Christmas by the time Vera returned home.

Garret wondered what had happened to the cool guy who was willing to buy him beer, but it was a passing thought, and soon even Garret forgot about the man. The teenager surprised his family by getting straight As on his report card. In spite of his academic achievements, he didn't abandon his wild ways.

At the Chamberlain house, Alex and Katie helped their mother decorate Christmas cookies while Tommy helped their father put up the Christmas tree. As the gifts began to appear around the tree, the three Chamberlain children fondled the colorful packages, making guesses as to the contents.

The FBI no longer believed Anthony Marino was in the Coulson or Clement Falls area, so they began looking elsewhere. While they continued to keep an eye on the Clement Falls boardinghouse, should Marino return to see his sister, they no longer had any interest in Coulson or its residents.

Up at Clement Falls, Gina Carracci grieved for the loss of her brother. Nick Carracci tried to be patient with his wife, yet was silently thankful Anthony Marino was out of their lives. Unlike his wife, he was not certain his brother-in-law was gone for good—but he prayed, each night, the man would never return.

AFTER 1961 ARRIVED, A NEW PRESIDENT, JOHN KENNEDY, WAS sworn into office. As the country rolled into the sixties, its landscape changed in ways Randall's bride, Mary Ellen Browning, would never have imagined. Coloring the decade was social unrest, a civil rights movement, a slain president, murdered civil rights leaders, and an unpopular war in Vietnam. Man was preparing to walk on the moon while back on earth hippies marched for peace and free love.

By the time Sonny returned from his European tour, he decided he no longer wanted to be called by his nickname but insisted on using his legal given name. It caused a certain amount of confusion sharing his father's name, but the family quickly adapted.

It didn't take long for Randall to realize his eldest grandson had no business aptitude, but he did have a flair for charming people. Randall kept Sonny moving, transferring him from one Coulson Enterprises location to another. The younger Harrison's responsibilities at the company were insignificant at best, which made the young man quite happy. The life of a roving playboy, who simply had to smile for the camera when the public relations department needed a pretty face, suited him well.

Garret left Coulson to attend college two months after graduating from high school. After completing his bachelor's, he went for his master's. Maintaining high grades was keeping him out of the draft and out of Vietnam, but he understood he might not be able to avoid the draft indefinitely.

In the fall of 1968, Russell Coulson was the last of the three brothers to still be living at Coulson House. Russell, Tommy, and Ryan were all juniors in high school—the same grade Garret had been in when he had saved Alexandra from the third-grade bullies. Alexandra and Jimmy started high school that fall. They had become close friends over the years, and Jimmy was no longer a pudgy first grader but a lean young man with a ready smile.

Wally Keller never remarried, but he had several lady friends over the years. He had remodeled the motel and business proved steady. It had been years since he had thought about Anthony Marino, and not a single motel guest reported seeing a ghost in room ten.

Up in Clement Falls, Gina Carracci passed away a few years after her brother's disappearance, leaving her husband to raise their young daughter alone. With Gina gone, there was no one left to ask—or care—about Anthony Marino's fate. Even the FBI had moved on, believing Marino must have pissed off one of his former employers and was wearing a pair of concrete boots. Since his disappearance, there had been no hits with his trademark touches. What those were exactly were never revealed—just in case he was still out there.

CHAPTER TWENTY-TWO

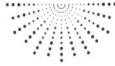

*R*eclining on her bed, Alexandra glanced up from the book she was reading and looked over at her sister, Katie.

"What in the hell are you doing?" Alexandra asked. Katie stood by the dresser, her blouse pulled up, as she shoved a sock in her bra.

"I'm going to the bathroom," Katie told her.

"Umm...you have to do that with a sock in your bra?" Alex asked.

Katie grabbed a second sock from her dresser drawer and shoved it in the other side of her bra. Pulling her blouse down, she looked in the mirror. Using her hands to rearrange and shape the sock-breasts, she ignored her sister's inquiry.

"Oh, now I get it," Alexandra said with a chuckle. She closed the book and set it on her lap. "Don't tell me, Tommy is home and he has some of his friends with him."

"So?" Katie leaned closer to the mirror and began applying makeup.

"You know Mom doesn't like you to wear makeup. And thanks for asking me if you can use mine, by the way."

"Well, it's not like I'm going anywhere. And why do you get to wear it and I can't? We're only a year apart."

"I don't know why Mom makes the rules she does. But please, Katie, don't go out there like that. You look silly."

"I do not!" Katie protested.

"You've obviously stuffed your bra. Please. Tommy's friends aren't worth it."

Katie paused for a moment and looked at her sister. Letting out a sigh, she slipped her hand under her blouse and removed the socks. Any illusion of breasts vanished.

"Don't you think Russell Coulson is cute?" Katie asked.

"He's too old for you."

"But don't you think he's cute?"

"I guess he's okay." Alexandra shrugged and started reading her book again.

"Gosh, Alex, what's the point of putting up with Tommy if we can't check out his cute friends?"

"Well, check out all you want. But don't parade yourself in front of them. Boys can be jerks. And trust me, when you start high school next year, you don't want to be known as Socks."

"Socks is kinda a cute name," Katie said brightly.

Alexandra lowered her book and glared at Katie. "*Really?*"

"Well," Katie said with a shrug, "I guess not if they're talking about my boobs." Walking to the bedroom door, she opened it slightly and peeked out. After a moment, she closed it and faced her sister.

"I wonder why they're home so early. It isn't past Tommy's curfew yet."

"Who knows? Who cares?" Alex asked, again focusing on her book.

"HEY, CHAMBERLAIN, I SAW YOUR SISTER AT SCHOOL TODAY." Ryan Keller lounged on Tommy's bed, looking up at the ceiling as he bounced a football in his hands.

"So?" Tommy sat at his desk, sharing a pizza with Russell.

"Just sayin'. You guys check out the new crop of freshmen? Some real dogs. Looks like Alex might be the pick of the litter this year."

"Don't be an ass." Tommy wadded up a soiled napkin and tossed it in Ryan's direction. It fell to the floor.

"Hey, it's true. If she wasn't your sister, I'd be tempted. Of course, she doesn't have boobs yet."

"Fuck, Keller." Tommy glared at Ryan. "Shut up already."

Ryan laughed, then tossed the ball at Tommy, who knocked it to the floor.

"I saw Alex at school today too," Russell commented. "And Jimmy. How did he do this week as a freshman? Any hazing?"

"Shit no. I told the guys if they touched my brother, I'd kick their ass," Ryan told him.

"Well, you touch my sister, and I'll kick yours," Tommy warned.

"No problem. I'd rather wait for her to get tits."

Tommy reached to the floor, grabbed the football and threw it at Ryan, who managed to grab it before it hit him.

Russell took his slice of pizza and sat on the floor, leaning against the side of the bed.

"Those guys were getting crazy tonight," Russell said. No longer a blond, Russell's hair had darkened like his older brothers'.

"Yeah, it was getting wild at the lake. I sure as hell didn't want to get busted. My dad would kill me," Ryan said.

"It was a good thing we left when we did," Tommy said.

"Yeah, I have to work tomorrow anyway." Ryan tossed the football to the floor.

"What shift? Can you go out tomorrow night?" Tommy asked.

"Morning shift. Flipping eggs. Let me crash for a couple hours after I get off, then I'll be ready to go." Ryan had been working at restaurants since he was twelve years old, beginning as a busboy.

"Cool. I have to work for a few hours at my dad's office but should be off by two. How about you, Coulson?" Tommy asked.

"Are you kidding, Russell doesn't have to work." Ryan laughed.

"Shut up, Chamberlain." Russell stood up and tossed his paper plate in the trash can.

"Sorry," Ryan said, still chuckling. "But it's true."

Before Russell could respond, the phone began to ring. Tommy answered it at the same time as Alex, and after a brief exchange, she hung up because the call was for Tommy.

"Fuck, no. You're kidding?" Tommy said into the phone. "So what happened?" Tommy was now sitting on the edge of his chair. "Who else was there? What are they going to do?"

Ryan and Russell listened attentively to Tommy's end of the conversation. It went on for several more minutes, and finally he hung up.

"Fuck," Tommy said when he hung up the phone. There were tears in his eyes.

"What happened?" Ryan asked, now sitting on the edge of the bed.

"The cops showed up at the lake to bust the party. Mike jumped in the water, not wanting to get busted. He never came up."

"What do you mean he never came up?" Russell asked.

"They think he drowned," Tommy said.

"No. He's just fucking with them. Mike's a great swimmer. He probably swam over to the other side of the lake and got out. I bet he's home now, laughing his ass off," Ryan insisted.

"He didn't come home."

"Well, shit, he probably had to walk there. He'll show up. You'll see," Ryan said.

BY SATURDAY MORNING, NEWS AROUND COULSON WAS THAT sixteen-year-old Mike Murphy had drowned in Sutter's Lake. They were sending divers to look for his body. Tommy's dad told him he didn't need to go in the office that day. Before noon, Russell picked up Tommy and the two teenagers drove down to Sutter's Lake to see what was going on.

Katie wanted to go with them, but her mother wouldn't let her. Alexandra had no desire to go to the lake. The last thing she wanted to witness was the lifeless body of one of her classmates being dragged from the icy water.

When Tommy and Russell got to the lake, the parking lot was full. Many of their classmates had the same idea. The officials didn't send the teenagers away but told them they had to keep to the north shore. Tommy and Russell found a dry place to sit and watch as the divers looked for their friend's body.

"This just totally sucks," Tommy said.

"I hope they don't find him. I hope he's just being an ass and fucking with us." Russell didn't take his eyes off the divers.

"I heard this lake is really deep. If he did drown, I hope they find him."

"Yeah, you're right. My dad said it's one of the deepest lakes in the state."

"I wish Mike would've listened and come home with us last night." Tommy wiped tears from his eyes.

"I know, but he was pretty wasted."

They heard someone shout, "I found something!" They were too far away to hear what was being said, and by the commotion, something was going on. They could see one of the police officers on his radio. In spite of the burst of activity, nothing was being pulled from the lake. After about fifteen minutes, a tow truck pulled up. They watched as it backed up to the lake, guided by two police officers.

"Why do they need a tow truck?" Tommy asked.

"Hell if I know."

While the tow truck backed up to the water, Russell pointed to the other side of the lake. "Look, they're still diving over there. What's going on?"

They looked back to the tow truck. It was slowly dragging something from the lake. They watched in fascination as a waterlogged 1958 Lincoln Continental Mark III gradually emerged from the water. Just as the car was removed from the lake, there was another shout from the other direction. They'd found Mike's body.

Tommy and Russell watched as their friend's lifeless

body was removed from the lake. In the distance, they could see Mike's parents and hear their cries of anguish. After members from the fire department loaded the body into a van, Mr. Murphy helped his wife to their car, and the two drove away, following the van from the parking lot.

"Fuck." Tommy wiped away more tears.

The two teenagers sat there for a few moments before finally standing up. Walking back to the parking lot, they noticed the small crowd around the car that had been pulled from the lake.

Silently, they approached the Lincoln Continental and listened to the chatter of the police officers, who were inspecting the vehicle.

"I've seen that car before," Tommy whispered.

"WELL, NOW WE KNOW WHAT HAPPENED TO ANTHONY Marino's car," Wally said as he read the Sunday paper. "Now the question I have, what happened to him?"

"Who was that again?" Jimmy asked. He poured syrup on his pancakes.

"The one who used to put candy in the mailbox," Ryan reminded his brother. The three sat around the Keller breakfast table.

"I liked that guy," Jimmy said.

"Yeah, you were like six. Wasn't he a hit man, Dad?" Ryan asked.

"That's what I heard." Wally folded the newspaper and tossed it aside, then added, "I'm really sorry about Mike. He was a good kid."

"Yeah, I remember when I used to watch you guys play

over-the-line," Jimmy told his brother, recalling the games at the park with Russell, Tommy, and Mike.

"When is the funeral?" Wally asked.

"I haven't heard. But this really sucks," Ryan said glumly.

A WEEK AFTER MIKE'S DEATH, RUSSELL, RYAN AND TOMMY downed a case of beer. In their drunken state, they solemnly vowed to be friends forever, and when the time came for one of them to join Mike, the two remaining friends would help carry the deceased's casket to its final resting place.

News of Marino's car being hauled from the lake, after it first went missing almost eight years earlier, might have received more press had the town not been grieving for one of its own. However, the discovery did attract the attention of Agents Carmichael and Stephens, who had always assumed Marino had left Coulson on his own volition.

The two agents now wondered if Marino was still alive, and if not, where was his body and who killed him? With Marino's sister gone and no known associates of Marino in Coulson—aside from a very casual and brief acquaintance with the town's founding family and the Kellers—they had no other leads.

CHAPTER TWENTY-THREE

*F*all turned to winter and winter to spring. Summer arrived again, and the cycle continued. As December of 1969 approached, another decade was coming to a close. Fighting continued in Vietnam, and Garret Coulson, who had returned to his hometown, was waiting for the results of the draft lottery to see where his future lay—in the military or Coulson Enterprises. When the numbers were drawn on December 1, 1969, it was safe to say his future was with Coulson Enterprises; his number was 342.

"You could always move back home," Vera told Garret. Christmas was three weeks away and the Coulson family was holding a celebratory dinner at one of the new seafood restaurants in town. The special occasion was Garret's high lottery number. Sonny was the only family member not in attendance, as he was currently living in Chicago.

"Really, Mother? That's a generous offer, thank you—but no. I've found an apartment."

"Well, it's going to be lonely there, with Russell leaving in the fall for college." Vera looked over to her youngest son.

Harrison was right when he had told Vera, *"We'll go back to how we were before. Before Anthony Marino came into our lives."* They continued to occupy separate bedrooms, and Vera didn't doubt he kept a mistress. She didn't invite Harrison to share her bed, nor did he ask. In public, no one doubted they were a couple, albeit not an affectionate one. No one considered that particularly odd.

Vera tried, in her own awkward way, to improve her relationship with her sons, but in many ways, they were strangers to her, so she wasn't sure how to progress. Of the three, Garret was the most distant and impossible to reach. At times, she suspected he hated her.

"I'd like to make a toast," Randall said as he raised his glass. "To the newest member of Coulson Enterprises... sorry, Uncle Sam, I'm keeping him!"

THE NEXT DAY GARRET WAS ALONE ON MAIN STREET, DOING A little shopping. His first stop was the diner for breakfast. When he finished eating, he planned to walk down the street to the furniture store and look at sofas.

A few moments after leaving the diner, a woman's voice called out, "Garret? Garret Coulson?"

Garret stopped walking and turned in the direction of the voice.

"Sheryl?" Garret said in surprise when he spied the young woman walking toward him. He hadn't seen her since he had graduated from high school. She didn't look much different than he remembered, just a little older and her hair was cut into an attractive style that did much more for her looks than how she had worn it in school.

167

"I thought that was you!" Sheryl gave him a welcoming hug, which he accepted and returned.

"You look great," Garret told her when their hug ended.

"I was about to say the same thing about you. God, it's been years!"

"You still live in Coulson?" Garret asked.

"Oh, hell no!" Sheryl laughed at the idea. "I left right after high school. I'm just visiting my mom for Christmas. Thought I'd do a little Christmas shopping. You?"

"I just moved back," Garret explained. "What are you up to these days?"

Sheryl flashed her left hand, showing her wedding band. "I married a very nice man I met in Colorado. We have a little girl."

"You look happy. Are you happy, Sheryl?"

She smiled up at him. "Yes, Garret, I am. Of course, I spent a shitload of money on a shrink after I left Coulson. But I finally got my head on straight. I'm in a good place now."

Garret smiled. "I'm glad to hear that. You really do look radiant."

"Probably because I'm expecting!" Sheryl laughed. Garret smiled again and gave her a quick hug.

"Garret," Sheryl began, her tone now serious, "I'm glad I ran into you today. I've always wanted to thank you for being so sweet to me back then."

"Hell, Sheryl, I'm older now and hopefully a little wiser. I realize now I would have been a hell of a lot better friend if I had kept our friendship...platonic."

"Don't be silly," Sheryl told him. Standing on her tiptoes, she kissed his cheek. "Sweetie, you were as fucked up as I was."

A FAMILIAR FACE ON THE MORNING'S NEWSPAPER CAUGHT Monica's eye as she was about to walk into the liquor store. She paused at the newsstand. It was already noon, and there was only one paper left in the rack. Digging in her purse, she found the necessary coins to make her purchase. After buying the newspaper, she opened it and walked into the liquor store, paying more attention to what was in the paper than her surroundings.

It was an excellent picture of Harrison. He was standing with his grandfather in front of the construction site by Coulson Enterprises' home office. When she got back to her apartment, she would have to cut it out and put it in her scrapbook. She didn't have a real photograph of him, just pictures taken from the local newspaper. He was funny about that. Once, she tried to snap his picture with her Instamatic camera and he about had a fit.

Walking over to the wine section, she picked up a bottle of Harrison's favorite wine. She hadn't seen him the night before. His excuse was some family gathering. Apparently, they were celebrating his middle son's lottery number. They —meaning his wife, father, and two youngest sons. She had never met Harrison's father before, yet she had heard enough about the man to know it wasn't an introduction she eagerly anticipated. Someday, Randall Coulson would be her father-in-law, so she couldn't avoid the man forever.

She had never seen the two older sons. It was a little strange to think one day she would have two stepsons older than herself. Although, she didn't think Garret was that much older. She had seen the youngest boy at a high school football game. Like the father, young Russell was a handsome man.

Monica had seen Vera Coulson around town. Harrison rarely mentioned his wife and never spoke ill of her, which irritated the shit out of Monica. Whenever Monica brought up the subject of Vera Coulson, Harrison told her his wife had nothing to do with their relationship and changed the subject.

"Did you read the article?" The cashier pointed to the one with Harrison, then rang up the wine.

"No, I just bought it." Monica didn't really care about the article. She just wanted the picture of Harrison.

"It's about the Garden Pavilion. That's what they're calling it," the teller explained. "They're remodeling the corporate offices and adding some modern-looking lobby. Making a big deal about it. I guess some hotshot architect from back east designed it. Looks like a tall glass box to me. Supposed to have it done by Christmas."

Monica didn't respond. She didn't tell the teller she had been to the inner offices of Coulson Enterprises and that she knew all about the Garden Pavilion. Instead, she quietly paid for her bottle of wine and left.

December 20, 1969, marked the grand opening of Coulson Enterprises' Garden Pavilion. The immense lobby, a combination of walnut panels and glass panes, cut into the sky above Coulson Enterprises' main offices. Early Saturday morning, the decorators arrived to put the final festive touches on the impressive lobby in time for the annual Christmas party.

While decorators laced ribbon and holly along the perimeter of the lobby and adorned the fragrant blue spruce in its center with shiny glass balls for the evening's bash, caterers set up tables and a bar.

At Coulson House, Randall refreshed himself for the evening's celebration with a nap. His driver took Vera to her beauty shop for an afternoon of pampering before the big event. Russell and Ryan managed to get in nine holes of golf. When they were done, Ryan dashed off to his restaurant job, while Russell went home to shower before picking up his date and going to the Christmas party. Garret, who had moved into his apartment weeks before, waited for the delivery of his new couch.

Meanwhile, Harrison Coulson was in his private office located in the original complex now attached to the Garden Pavilion. He was not alone.

———

MONICA INSISTED SHE LOVED HIM. BUT HARRISON WAS NOT A fool; he was twice her age. Twenty-five-year-old girls typically did not seek out much older men from lust or love. It was money and power that stoked their passion.

In the early days of his affairs, beginning after Russell's birth, Harrison gravitated toward women closer to his own age. Monica was his first much younger woman.

He had severed the relationship with his last mistress six months earlier. It was Monica who sought his attention—in much the same way Vera had thirty years earlier. He found her seduction hard to resist.

"I wish I could come with you tonight," Monica told him as she stood in the center of his office, unbuttoning her white silk blouse. Harrison lounged lazily against his desk, watching her undress.

"You know that's impossible." His gaze swept over her body.

"I understand. I was just saying..." She slipped off her blouse and laid it over his office chair.

"I could get you a job tonight—with our caterer."

"Caterer?" She unhooked her bra, freeing her plump breasts. Harrison stared at the rosy nipples, admiring the ample spheres, so soft yet so firm. He liked that they didn't sag. *You can't beat youth,* Harrison told himself.

"Yes, you could wear one of those cute little serving outfits. Very short skirts, frilly panties. It might be exciting; we could slip away for a quick fuck when the party is in full swing."

"I hate it when you're crude," Monica said, wiggling out of her skirt.

"That's what we do, Monica, we fuck." Harrison reached over on his desk and picked up his cigar.

"Do you have to smoke that?" Monica asked, now standing before him wearing just her panties.

"As a matter of fact, I do." Harrison bit off the tip of the cigar and spit it in the trash can.

"Why are you being so mean to me?"

He wasn't sure why he was such a prick, but she pissed him off. "You think I am being mean?"

"Sort of," Monica said in a quiet voice.

"Do you want to leave?"

"Do you want me to?" Tears filled her eyes.

"I don't want you to do anything you don't want to do." He pulled a lighter out of his pocket and lit his cigar. Smoke curled around his face.

"Harrison, I just want to do what makes you happy. I love you."

"I'm sorry, Monica. I don't mean to be a bastard. I don't know what's gotten into me today."

"I understand, Harrison. It's okay."

Harrison set his cigar in the ashtray on the desk. Unzipping his pants, he took his penis in his hand while sitting back in the large leather chair.

"Then take off those panties and show me how you want to make me happy."

THE FURNITURE COMPANY DELIVERED GARRET'S COUCH earlier than expected, which freed up his Saturday afternoon. He decided to use the time to set up his new office at Coulson Enterprises. He would have plenty of time to return to his apartment to get ready for the Christmas party.

Along with the construction of the Garden Pavilion, the existing offices had been remodeled. Garret hadn't had a chance to orient himself to the complex's layout, which explained why he wasn't sure if he turned down the correct hallway to get to his office. The doors all looked the same to him.

He had misplaced the key to his new office, so the day before he had asked his grandfather where he might get a spare. Randall had tossed him a key ring and said, "One of these is for your office. I'm not sure which one."

Garret was fairly certain he had turned down the right corridor and was standing at the door to his office. He wasn't sure which key would fit the door, so he decided to just start trying every key until he found the one that worked. To his surprise, the first key slipped in and unlocked the door. Smiling, he pushed it open.

The sight that awaited him was not what he expected. It

wasn't his office he had just entered—but his father's. It wasn't empty, and his father was not alone.

Harrison Coulson, his pants off, sat on a leather chair with his knees spread apart as a buxom young blonde bounced energetically up and down on his penis. Her back was to her lover as her enormous breast jiggled and bobbed, reminding Garret of some grotesque dirty cartoon.

The pair was unaware of the audience and vocal in their pleasure. Harrison grabbed hold of the bouncing orbs, squeezing roughly, as he pulled her closer.

Holding his breath, Garret eased from the room, closing the door behind him. Instead of looking for his office, he went back to his apartment. Garret never imagined his father was faithful to his mother. His parents didn't share a bedroom, and while he remembered some affection between the two when he was a small child, that seemed to stop after Russell's birth.

Witnessing Harrison cheating on his mother angered Garret more than he would have expected had someone told him what he was about to see. His father's lover was a beautiful woman. But she was far too young, and he found something perverse in such a wide age gap. The thought of a man Harrison's age and wealth seducing a girl that looked to be around Garret's own age was offensive to him.

He wasn't sure how he would react when he saw his father at the Christmas party. He also wondered...who was she?

GARRET STROLLED THROUGH THE CROWD OF PARTY GUESTS, A scotch in hand, as he chatted amicably with one person and then another. Because of his height and broad shoulders, it was impossible to find a properly fitting tux off the rack. He wore one that had been tailor made for the party. By the reaction of the women in attendance, it was money well spent. To the delight of the single ladies—and a few married ones, he hadn't brought a date.

He was wondering which one of the lovely ladies he would take home with him when he spied *her*—the woman his father had been vigorously screwing several hours earlier. She carried a tray with champagne glasses and, like the other servers who worked for the caterer, wore a sexy little French maid outfit.

Dad is fucking the help? Garret thought. He watched as she moved toward Harrison and Vera. Boldly, the woman offered his mother a glass of champagne. Vera paid little attention to the server and continued to talk to one of her friends as she took a glass from the tray. He watched his father, whose hand slipped under the woman's short skirt for a brief second to cop a feel.

Incensed at the display, Garret decided to teach Harrison a lesson. Forcing a smile, he walked directly to his father.

"Congratulations, Dad, the new lobby looks amazing," Garret told Harrison as his eyes followed his father's mistress.

"Thanks, Garret, your grandfather and I are very pleased with how it turned out."

"And I must say," Garret whispered under his breath, "the caterer you hired has some tasty little pieces." He nodded toward Monica.

"Yes, she is an attractive girl," Harrison said as he took a sip of his drink.

"Well, at least I know who I'm taking home tonight," Garret whispered to Harrison.

"What are you talking about?"

"Her." Garret nodded toward Monica again.

"Don't be ridiculous. You're the one always saying employees should be off-limits as sexual conquests."

"The company may have hired the caterer, but technically speaking, she really doesn't work for Coulson. I'd make an exception for her."

"Leave her alone. She's working," Harrison snapped.

"Later, Dad. I need to go line up my midnight snack." Garret walked away, leaving his father fuming.

CHAPTER TWENTY-FOUR

"*H*aving fun?" Garret asked Monica twenty minutes later. She stood at the edge of the dance floor, holding an empty tray. It appeared as if she was looking for someone in the crowd, *Harrison perhaps?*

Startled, Monica turned to face Garret. "Well, not really. This isn't how I expected to spend my evening."

Garret brushed the side of her face with his fingertips. Guileless blue eyes looked back at him. He was fairly certain his father was somewhere watching. "You could come home with me. I promise you'll have a much better time."

"Who are you?" She thought he looked like a much younger version of Harrison.

"My name is Garret, Garret Coulson."

"I...I need to go." Monica started to walk away.

"No, come with me first. I'd like to show you something."

Without giving her a chance to resist, Garret took the serving tray from her hand and placed it on a nearby table. He then grabbed her wrist and began leading her toward a door. Monica looked around frantically but let Garret lead her out of the lobby and into a secluded hallway.

"Where are you taking me?" she asked.

"I just want to talk to you. It's awful noisy in there."

"What do you want to talk about?"

When they were alone in the hallway, Garret released her and asked, "What do you see in him?"

"I don't know what you mean," she said, her voice wavering.

"My father."

"How do you know?" she whispered guiltily.

"It doesn't matter. How old are you?"

She didn't answer immediately. Finally, she said, "Twenty-five."

"Good lord, you're my age! He's married. Do you think he's going to leave my mother?"

"I love him."

"Fuck." Garret rubbed his forehead. "Has he made you any promises?"

"Promises?"

"Did he say he was going to leave my mother?"

"Please don't hate me," Monica begged. "But I love your father; I can make him happy."

"I'm going to warn you—if you have any grand ideas of getting pregnant, trying to force him to leave my mother to marry you, he had a vasectomy. He can't get you pregnant."

Monica didn't respond. She hadn't known he'd had a vasectomy; they had never discussed it. But when they first started their affair Harrison refused to use a condom, telling her not to worry about it; he was taking care of things. She thought that meant he would marry her if she got pregnant. In fact, she assumed that was what he secretly wanted—for her to get pregnant and then he would be able to end his loveless marriage.

"What's your name?"

"Monica."

"How did you meet my father?"

"Are you going to tell your mother about me?"

"No."

"I was a cocktail waitress at the Roseville."

"So Dad picked you up there?" Garret was disgusted.

"No, it wasn't your father's fault. He was always so nice to me, so charming. He never made any advances. I promise. He used to come into the bar with another woman, but not your mother. I'd seen your mother before." She paused for a moment.

"Go on."

"Well, I was working and I overheard your father break up with her. He told her she was getting too serious and that he didn't want that kind of relationship. When she left the bar, I approached him."

"What do you mean?"

"I told him I'd had a crush on him forever, and if he ever wanted to go out—or whatever, I would be there. No strings."

"Is it his money?"

"No!" She sounded insulted. "I love your father. Your mother doesn't love him. I can tell. When I see them together, she never touches him. I'm sorry. I know she's your mother. But I knew I could make him happy. And I do."

"How long has this been going on?"

"Do you hate me?"

"No. But I don't know why you'd care."

"You're Harrison's son."

"So?"

"Well, if Harrison ever left your mother...I would be your stepmother."

"Monica, you're wasting your life on my father. I seriously doubt he's going to leave my mother. For one thing, my grandfather does not believe in divorce, and if you know anything about my family, you'd know my father doesn't cross his father."

"I don't know about any of that. I just know how I feel."

"I'm going back to the party now. I've said all I have to say. For your own good, I wish you'd reconsider this relationship. It's not good for you." Without saying another word, Garret returned to the party.

***

AFTER GARRET LEFT, MONICA LINGERED IN THE HALLWAY alone, considering all that had been said. Before she had a chance to return to the lobby, Harrison burst into the hallway, clearly angry.

"What the fuck were you doing with my son in the hallway all this time?"

"Nothing, Harrison. Just talking, honest."

"Talking about what?"

"Nothing important."

"Are you fucking my son?"

"I just met him!" Tears filled her eyes.

"Don't lie to me."

"Please, Harrison, don't talk to me like that. I love you. I didn't do anything with your son. I was just trying to be friendly."

"I pay for your apartment; I give you a very generous allowance. So I don't expect you to screw around, especially with my son."

For the first time in their relationship, Monica felt like a whore—bought and paid for by the mighty Harrison Coulson. In spite of her feelings, she didn't want Harrison to be mad at her. She reached out for his hand, but he pushed her away and left her standing alone in the hallway.

CHAPTER TWENTY-FIVE

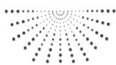

*S*tanding in the sunroom, Harrison gazed out the window while drinking his morning coffee. Heavy dark clouds filled December's sky.

"Harrison, you aren't ready for church." Vera's voice interrupted his solitude.

He turned to face her. Already dressed for church, she fit a pair of white gloves on her hands.

"I'm not going this morning." Still wearing his robe, he took another sip of coffee and turned back to face the window.

"What do you mean you aren't going? We always go." Vera stepped closer, now standing at his side by the window. "I didn't realize you'd had that much to drink last night."

"I didn't," he said.

"But I did wonder where you disappeared to for a while. That was until I saw you coming from the hallway leading to the offices. I wondered what I was missing, seemed like an active place. First Garret drags that waitress there; then he returns and you take his place. Sharing women with your son now, Harrison? Seems a bit tawdry."

"Your relationship with Garret seems to have improved recently. Might I suggest you not say this to him, or you'll be back to where you two were when he was in high school."

"Oh, I'm not really concerned about my relationship with our son. Your relationship with him is another matter."

"Don't worry, dear, I'm not sharing anything with Garret. I've never been one to share my toys, especially with my son." Harrison continued to look out the window and did not turn to his wife.

"I'm going to church with Randall and Russell." Vera turned and left the room.

What is wrong with me? Harrison asked himself. His behavior with Monica the day before was inexcusable. He had always prided himself on treating women with respect —even those who were casual bed partners. For some reason, Monica got under his skin, with her childlike blue eyes and constantly professing her undying love for him.

Glancing briefly at the doorway his wife had just exited, it suddenly dawned on him. *Monica reminds me of Vera!* Not the Vera now, but the Vera he'd met when he was still a green boy—*a virgin.*

Chicago 1936

HARRISON DIDN'T UNDERSTAND WHY ALL THE MEN IN THE room weren't staring at her. He couldn't take his eyes off the beautiful young woman in the green dress. The manner in which she tilted her head back as she laughed gaily, obviously amused by something the gentleman at her side was telling her, was utterly charming. Harrison would gladly trade his annual allowance to switch places with the man.

"Dad, who's that?" Harrison asked, nodding to the girl in

the green dress. It was crowded at the reception, so Randall wasn't sure which girl his son was referring too.

"The pretty redhead," Harrison whispered.

"Oh, that's Vera Chalmers. Her father's a business associate of mine." Randall smiled, noting his son's interest. "I wouldn't mind you pursuing that one, Harrison. Good family. Excellent connections. She's a bit older than you, but you're a mature lad."

"Oh, she would never be interested in someone like me." Harrison was just seventeen.

"Come, I'll introduce you."

An hour later, Harrison found himself alone in the garden with the lovely Miss Vera Chalmers. Muted sounds of laughter, conversation, and music drifted out from the open window.

"I was hoping they would introduce us," Vera said shyly, looking downward as they strolled along the garden path. Overhead, the full moon lit their way.

"You were?" Harrison could feel his palms sweat, he was so nervous. *She noticed me!*

"Oh yes. I've seen you before at the theater, with your parents." Vera flashed a coy smile. Harrison couldn't believe he had never noticed her before. Stammering, he didn't know what to say.

"My father tells me your mother has a most impressive library," Vera said. No longer walking, the two stood side by side under the moonlight.

"You like to read?"

"Some books I find fascinating," Vera whispered.

"It seems my mother is always reading a book. I prefer doing something rather than sitting with a book." He paused a moment. "Oh, I'm sorry. I didn't mean to imply there was anything wrong if you like to read."

"I understand. I used to find books very boring. But then a friend...well, he gave me books to read. I think you'd like them. I wonder...perhaps your mother has books like them in her library."

"I suppose. Mother has hundreds of books. The library used to belong to my uncle William."

"Your mother's brother?" Vera asked.

"No, he wasn't a real uncle. He was Dad's business partner. When he died, he left Mother his library.

"Oh, I would love to see it."

"Well, my parents are leaving for New York in the morning. Perhaps when they return, I can arrange it."

"How long are they going to be gone?" Vera asked.

"Two weeks, I believe," Harrison said.

"Oh...that's too bad. I wish I could see it sooner," Vera said with a pout.

Harrison did not want to wait two weeks to see the lovely Miss Vera. "I suppose I could show you. What day would be good for you?"

"Oh, thank you!" Vera said excitedly. "I could come over Wednesday afternoon."

"Okay, Wednesday it is."

"I have something I would like to send you, a book. Perhaps you could read it before Wednesday, and let me know what you think about it."

"A book?" Harrison wasn't thrilled about having to read a book, but he wanted to see Vera again.

"I have a feeling you may like it. But you must keep it a secret. And don't let anyone see it. It might get us in trouble."

"Why?" Harrison said.

"Oh, some people just don't understand." Vera shrugged. "But I hope you will."

On Monday morning, a package was delivered to Harrison's home. He took it and raced upstairs to see what Vera had sent him. Perhaps she included a note, he wondered, more excited about that possibility than having to read a boring book. But there was no note. He read the book's title, *The Life and Adventures of Miss Fanny Hill.* Opening it, Harrison began to read.

It was nothing like he expected—nothing like he had ever read before. Written in first person, it told the sexual exploits of young Frances Hill. Orphaned, she finds herself in London, where a madame attempts to profit on the young girl's virginity. Frances, or Fanny as she is called, is saved from giving her virginity to a repugnant older man and instead gives it to Charles, who is the love of her life.

Harrison was unable to put the book down. Finding it hard to believe Vera had actually read the explicit story, he wondered if somehow she had sent the wrong book. After he finished reading, he hid it in his room, not wanting one of the household staff to find it. That evening, he brought it out again to reread the passages he found most titillating.

"So you read the book?" Vera asked Wednesday afternoon as Harrison showed her up the stairway to the library. They were alone in the townhouse.

"Yes. Who gave it to you?" Harrison asked.

"A friend," Vera said.

"What friend?" Harrison wondered who had given her such a book.

"It doesn't matter, he died several months ago."

They entered the library.

"Have you shared that book with anyone else?"

"Oh no!" Vera gasped as if she found the suggestion horrifying. "You're the first one I've ever shared the book with. I thought you would understand. I saw how you looked at me."

Harrison's gaze fixed on Vera; she was even more beautiful than he remembered. He had never met a girl like her before.

"Didn't you like the story?" Vera whispered, sounding unsure.

"Well, yes. I...I suppose it was difficult not to like it. But...well...I understand why we need to keep it a secret."

"Sometimes," Vera whispered, "I pretend I'm Fanny."

"You do?" His erection pushed out the front of his trousers.

"We could play a game...perhaps pretend I'm Fanny and you're Charles. Would you like that?" Vera reached out and gently touched the front of his trousers, feeling his hardness. Harrison froze. No girl had ever touched him there.

That afternoon, on the floor of his mother's library, Harrison lost his virginity. So intoxicated by the sensual world Vera opened for him, he didn't ask who had taught her such erotic games. While his parents were in New York, they found time each day to sneak away to the library.

By the time his parents returned from New York, Harrison and Vera were publically seeing each other—yet her parents assumed the young man was courting their daughter and never imagined the two took every opportunity to re-enact the sexual exploits of Fanny Hill.

Only Mary Ellen, Harrison's mother, was uncomfortable with the courtship, believing Vera had set a trap for her young son. Mary Ellen broached the subject with Harrison, who told her not to worry; he intended to stay a bachelor like his uncle William.

By that time, Harrison's boyish crush had faded. No longer did he see Vera as a girl he would court—or ever marry—but he could not resist the sexual favors she freely and frequently offered. In his naiveté or lustful blindness, he believed she was doing something to prevent pregnancy.

His newly discovered sexual prowess gave him a sense of power and confidence. While his friends only fantasized of such sexual games or paid women for the privilege, lovely Vera had turned her body over to him—submitted to his will—encouraged him to use her in any way he desired. For a seventeen-year-old boy, he could not imagine anything better.

The price for his pleasure was paid on his wedding day. There was no way his father would allow him to shirk his duty. Vera came from one of the finest families in Chicago, and she was carrying his child. Through it all, she professed her love for Harrison.

CHAPTER TWENTY-SIX

*H*arrison set his empty coffee cup on the table. Turning from the window, he made his way upstairs to his bedroom. He needed to get dressed so he could see Monica.

An hour later, he stood before her apartment. Since he was paying her rent, he didn't hesitate to use his key to open the door. But it would be his last time, he told himself. Before leaving the estate, he had called to let her know he was on his way over.

"Harrison!" Monica excitedly greeted him. She wore a transparent floor-length robe; it clearly revealed the outline of her body. Putting his hand out, he blocked her from coming closer. She frowned at his snub and stepped back.

"What's wrong?" she asked with a pout.

Harrison stared at her for a moment. He wasn't certain when he realized the truth about his wife, perhaps when she was pregnant with Russell or before. It was easier to blame her for the socially unacceptable behavior—promiscuity a man couldn't resist but was ready to scorn. While he never knew the details, he was certain the man who had given her the book had also taken her virginity—seduced her—or even raped her. He had never asked. But now, with the benefit of years and maturity, he understood her far better than he had during the first years of their marriage.

He saw Vera in Monica—and he was the man with the book. Perhaps he had not initially seduced her—he was not her first—but he was twice her age, and he told himself it had to stop.

"Monica, you're a beautiful young woman, but I'm wrong for you. I don't love you, and you need to be with someone who cares about you."

"No!" Monica cried out, throwing herself at his feet. Harrison stood stoically, looking down at the sobbing young woman.

"I'll pay your rent for the next six months and put a little something in your bank account. But it's over."

"No!" She clung desperately to his legs. Looking up at him, tears streamed down her face. "I promise, whatever you want I'll do. Just tell me what I did wrong. Was it the fact I talked to your son? I won't ever do that again!"

He leaned down and gently, yet firmly, untangled her hold and stepped back.

"Don't leave me, Harrison. I love you!"

"You don't love me, Monica. You don't even know me. You don't need to be with someone who treats you like I do. And I don't need to be the man I am when I'm with you."

Harrison turned and walked to the door. He paused a moment before leaving and set his key to her apartment on a table.

———

MONICA REFUSED TO GET DRESSED ON SUNDAY AND SPENT THE

rest of the afternoon alone in her apartment. She had no friends in Coulson, having moved to the town a month before meeting Harrison. There was no one she could call.

Watching television and eating ice cream from her bed, she cursed the day she had ever met Harrison Coulson. She loved the bastard, but he had dumped her, and she had no idea why. The tears had finally stopped, but her eyes were still puffy. Eventually, she fell asleep, not waking up until Monday afternoon.

Having nowhere to go, Monica spent most of Monday in her apartment. By nightfall, her anger over the breakup renewed and she cursed herself. Pissed, she decided to go drown her sorrows. Since there was no booze in her house and she didn't want to drink alone, she decided to go to a bar. There was no way she would go to the Roseville; Harrison liked to hang out there. With her luck, she would run into him and his wife.

She remembered seeing a new bar in town—the Tavern, located in the center of town. It was close to her apartment, which would allow her to walk home should she have too much to drink. Determined to put the bad love affair behind her, she picked out her sexiest dress and slipped it on.

GARRET DOWNED HIS SCOTCH AND ORDERED ANOTHER. He liked this new bar. One advantage, he doubted the Tavern would suit his father's tastes. He wished he didn't like his job at Coulson Enterprises so much; it would make it easier to tell the old man to shove it and find something else. The only problem, unlike his older brother, he really did like his hometown. Professional opportunities were scarce in Coulson. It was either work for Coulson Enterprises or move to a larger city.

He glanced up when the front door opened and someone walked in. He could tell it was a woman, but the dim lighting made it difficult to see her face. Turning back to the bartender, who had just brought him his second drink, he didn't notice the woman was walking toward him. It wasn't until she sat next to him and he turned in her direction did he see who it was. It was his father's mistress.

She seemed oblivious as to who was sitting next to her when she ordered a martini. Smiling, she turned in his direction. The smile quickly faded.

"You!" she accused. "I can't believe it!"

"Are you meeting my father here? Just tell me and I'll leave."

"No, I'm not meeting your asshole father here!" She stood up and looked at the bartender. "I'm going over to that booth. Please bring my drink there." Without saying another word to Garret, she grabbed her purse and stormed off to the dimly lit booth in the far corner of the bar. Curious, he turned on his barstool and looked over at Monica.

"What did she say?" the bartender asked, holding the martini he had just prepared.

"Here," Garret said as he took the drink. "I'll take it to her. Just put it on my tab." With his other hand, he picked up his scotch and strolled across the room to the booth.

Monica glared at Garret as he set the martini on the table before her.

"Thank you," she snapped, not sounding as if she meant it. Garret sat down in the booth with her.

"I didn't ask you to join me." She scooted over, away from Garret. He settled in and took a sip of his scotch.

"So what happened with you and the old man?"

"You'll be happy to know your father dumped me yesterday." She took a gulp of the martini.

"No kidding. How come? Did he find a replacement?"

"Oh, shut up." She took another gulp.

"Well, you're better off. He's too old for you."

"How do you know what's good for me?" This time she sipped the martini.

Eyeing him suspiciously, she said, "Hey, did you say something to him?"

"What do you mean?"

"About me. What we talked about Saturday night."

"No. I told you I wouldn't."

"Well, you must have said something," she insisted.

"He saw me go with you into the hallway. Later he asked me what happened. I told him I tried hitting on you, and you turned me down. That was all. I didn't let him know I knew about you two."

"Strange." Monica finished her martini. "When he came into the hall after you, he acted all jealous. Wanted to know what I'd done with you. He got all pissed. I sorta figured that meant he really cared."

"It was probably because it was me," Garret suggested, finishing the rest of his drink. He motioned to the bartender to bring them another round.

"He definitely did not like the idea of me and you."

"See, you should've taken me up on my offer." He chuckled.

"You mean when you asked me to come home with you?"

Garret nodded.

"Yeah, but you didn't mean it."

"You'd be amazed at what I do to piss off my father."

The drinks arrived. They discussed ways to piss off

Harrison. More drinks arrived. They laughed about pissing off Harrison and ways it might be accomplished. More drinks arrived.

How Garret actually managed to contact Randall's pilot and convince the man to fly Monica and himself to Las Vegas was unclear. He would remember there was a lot of giggling and laughter. He imagined it had to do with money, considering his wallet was empty by the time they had returned from Vegas the next morning.

Instead of going back to his or Monica's apartment, the newlyweds made their drunken way to Coulson House. Monica could not fully appreciate her first visit to the mansion, considering all the booze she had consumed.

———

THEY FOUND THE PAIR IN THE MORNING, SLEEPING ON THE living room sofa, the stench of stale cigarettes, gin, and scotch fouling the air. On the coffee table next to the sofa, in plain sight for all to see, was their wedding license.

Still a little drunk when roused from his slumber, Garret rubbed his eyes with the back of his hand; the room was spinning. Standing over him was his mother, father, and grandfather. Someone was sleeping on his legs. He looked down, trying to bring into focus the blond head sharing the couch with him.

Garret moved his legs, causing Monica to wake up. Through bleary bloodshot blue eyes, she looked at the people standing over her. Clearly horrified, she latched onto Garret's arm, desperately wanting him to shield her.

"What the fuck have you done to my son?" Harrison roared. Monica winced and Garret, now sitting up, protectively wrapped his arm around his bride's shoulders.

"Stop yelling, Dad," Garret told him. Squinting his eyes, his head pounded.

Ignoring Garret's request, Harrison continued to shout —hurling obscenities at Monica—calling her a scheming bitch and whore. Vera ran upstairs in tears while Randall attempted to get everyone to calm down. Monica was now crying, and Garret shouted back at his father. Randall managed to get between his son and grandson, telling Garret he needed to go until his father calmed down.

"I'M GOING TO KILL THAT BITCH," HARRISON FUMED TO HIS father. The pair sat in the library. Garret and Monica were no longer at Coulson House, and Vera was still in her room, crying. Russell had slept through the drama, yet it didn't take much effort to get the story from one of the kitchen staff who had overheard the ruckus.

"No, Harrison. You are going to calm down. The boy will simply get it annulled." Randall sat stoically in his leather chair while Harrison paced the room in a fit of agitation.

"Why aren't you upset?" Harrison asked.

"If I'm upset with anyone, it's you, Harrison. She was your mistress. You initially brought her into this family, Garret didn't. What were you thinking getting her a job with the caterer during the Christmas party?"

Sheepishly, Harrison looked at his father. "You're right. I was foolish. That's why I broke it off the next day. I realized it was out of control."

"Would have been nice had you broken it off *before* the Christmas party."

"I'm sorry, Dad. I'm going to go upstairs and speak to Vera."

Harrison found his wife upstairs in her bedroom, sitting on the side of her bed. She had stopped crying but was drying the corners of her eyes with a tissue. She looked up when he walked into her room.

"Are you okay?" Harrison asked.

"She was your mistress, wasn't she?" Vera asked.

"Yes."

"Younger than the others, Harrison." Vera took a deep breath then exhaled.

"I broke it off with her."

"Well, I would assume so." She glared up at her husband. "*Since she's now our daughter-in-law!*"

CHAPTER TWENTY-SEVEN

arret knocked on Monica's apartment door. It had been over forty-eight hours since his parents and grandfather had discovered them on the sofa. He hadn't seen Monica since dropping her off at her apartment after leaving Coulson House.

"I was wondering when you'd come by," Monica said after opening the front door. "Come on in."

Garret followed her into the living room.

"You want a cup of coffee?" she asked before sitting on the couch.

"No, thanks." Garret looked around the room. He knew his father had paid for her apartment.

"I still have a headache. How about you? Go ahead, sit down," Monica told him. She wore denims and a T-shirt. With her blond hair pulled back in a ponytail, she looked even younger than before.

"Thanks." Garret sat down.

"So is your dad still screaming? I was really afraid he would come over here."

"I don't think he will. I told him not to bother you."

"So what are we going to do?" Monica asked.

"Well, my grandfather and father have been on my case all day about getting the marriage annulled."

"Yeah, I figured that. Umm...I have a question...did we... you know...have sex?" Monica asked.

"You don't remember?"

"No, it's all kind of a blur."

"Well, not after we said our vows. But before, at the airport...in the car...while waiting for the pilot. Yeah. Sorry."

"Oh fuck." Monica rubbed her temple with the heel of her hand.

"I'm sorry, Monica. Honestly."

"It isn't your fault. I'm as much to blame. Did you use a condom?"

"We did, but I seem to recall it fell off in the middle of things. We were rather...umm...anxious to continue. I don't remember a second one."

"Can we still get an annulment since we had sex?"

"I don't know. But I think we should wait. Just in case you're pregnant."

"If I'm pregnant, your father is going to kill me."

"Fuck my father."

"I did that already. That's what got me into this mess."

"WHEN DO I GET TO MEET YOUR WIFE?" RUSSELL ASKED Garret. It was Saturday and the two brothers were playing golf.

"I told you, you aren't going to meet her. And I hope you aren't telling people I got married." Garret climbed into the golf cart, waiting for his brother to join him.

"No, but I heard it from Regina." Russell climbed into the cart.

"She's the new girl working in the kitchen?" Garret steered the cart to the next hole.

"Yeah. I have a feeling she likes to talk."

"Well, she won't keep her job long. You know how Mom is about the staff gossiping about family business."

"I know. So what's the deal? Dad says it was just one of your stunts, and you're getting it annulled."

"Dad doesn't know shit."

"So do you love her?"

"Russell, can we please talk about something else?"

———

"I'M NOT PREGNANT," MONICA TOLD GARRET WHEN HE arrived at her apartment on Sunday.

"You sure?" Garret asked.

Monica rolled her eyes and showed Garret into the apartment. "So are your parents freaking out about us still not doing anything about the marriage?"

"Pretty much." Garret sat with Monica in the living room. "I swear, if I hear my father say annulment one more time, I'm going to stay married to you.

"Well, I think I have something to say about that."

"What do you plan to do—after?" Garret asked.

"Leave Coulson. There's nothing for me here. But I confess...this may sound strange...but I wish we could get a divorce instead of an annulment."

Garret's inquisitive expression startled her.

"Oh no, I am not saying that because I want alimony or anything. Honest. I don't want anything from you. This was my fault as much as yours. Annulments...well, I always thought they were something people got who wanted a free pass to have sex."

"That...well, is a little odd...considering..."

"Considering I was sleeping with your father? Yeah, I know," Monica admitted.

"Actually, I'd be okay with a divorce. Might take a little longer."

"Is that because your father wants you to get an annulment?"

"What do you think?" Garret asked.

"You wanted to talk to me, Grandfather?" Garret asked as he entered Randall's office at Coulson Enterprises.

"Yes, go ahead and sit down, Garret."

Garret took the chair facing Randall's desk.

"I've been pleased with your work here. I'm very impressed."

"Thank you." Garret smiled.

"Now, if we could just get your private life in order." Randall eyed his grandson with keen interest.

"Is this about the annulment again? If so, I think I'll get back to work." Garret started to stand up.

"No, sit down, young man. I'll tell you when you can go."

With a sigh, Garret sat back down.

"I want you to know I blame your father more than you."

"You do?" Garret was surprised.

"I know your grandmother was upset when your father married your mother. I suppose the conditions weren't ideal."

"Because she was pregnant with Harrison?"

"Things like that happen. And it worked out. She gave

him three sons. Three fine sons. That's quite an accomplishment."

"Even if I'm one of those sons?" Garret asked.

"I'll admit you've been the wildest of the bunch. But you might end up being the smartest. That is, of course, if you can stop doing stupid things."

Garret laughed.

"So are you going to get an annulment, or are you going to stay in this marriage to punish your father?"

"Is that what I'm doing?" Garret asked.

"Isn't it?"

Garret shrugged. "I was thinking of getting a divorce."

"Divorce? Why? I imagine that would take longer and cost more money. But if you keep putting it off, it might end up being your only option."

"I have my reasons, Grandfather."

"It might mean alimony. You don't want that."

"She doesn't want any."

"What does she intend to do after the marriage ends? Is she staying in town?"

"She says she wants to leave. I don't know where she intends to go."

They were silent for a few moments as Randall considered the situation.

"I'll tell you what. Let me talk to my attorney, get the divorce going. I'll cover all the expenses—he'll make sure you won't have any future support problems. And I'll give her a settlement to help her start a new life."

"Why would you do that, Grandfather?"

"You're my grandson, Garret. I protect what's mine."

"Can we not tell my father...until it's over?"

"You want to let him stew about it longer?" Randall asked.

"I suppose."

"Fine. It'll be between us. Harrison doesn't have to know the details. When the divorce is final, you can tell your father."

"Okay. But I'm going to tell my mother this afternoon," Garret told him.

"That might be a good idea."

GARRET'S ARRIVAL AT COULSON HOUSE SURPRISED VERA. Sitting in the sunroom reading a magazine when he arrived, she was the only member of the family at home. It was the first time they had seen each other since she had found him on the couch with Monica.

"Garret." Vera closed the magazine and set it on her lap. "I'm surprised to see you. How are you...how is your wife?"

"That's why I'm here, Mother. We need to talk."

Vera nodded and then tossed the magazine on the floor. She watched as Garret took the chair across from her.

"I didn't mean to hurt you," he said.

"I don't blame you."

"I've been hearing that a lot lately," he said under his breath.

"Excuse me?" She hadn't heard what he had said.

"It doesn't matter. I want to explain what happened and why."

"Are you staying married to this woman?"

"No. But for now, I would appreciate it if you not say anything to Dad. Grandfather is arranging a divorce, and Monica has agreed to everything. She wants out of this fake marriage as much as I do. She plans to leave town."

"Why not an annulment?"

"We have our reasons, but that's not important. I just want to tell you why it happened."

"I think I can guess," Vera told him. "Your father broke it off with her, you two—for whatever reason—got drunk together and came up with the brilliant idea of getting married to punish your father."

"Wow. That pretty much sums up the situation."

They were silent for a few moments.

"I wonder," Vera said sadly, "why can't our family have normal marriages?"

"Normal? I'm not sure what you mean."

"Like other couples I see. Happy marriages, where they are both friends and lovers. It seems impossible in this family."

"Well, there was Grandfather and Grandma Mary Ellen."

Vera reached out and briefly touched her son's knee. "Your grandmother never liked me. I suppose I can understand why. She always believed I had some devious plans for her only son. But the fact was, her marriage with your grandfather was peculiar. Perhaps just as peculiar as mine... and yours."

"I don't understand what you're saying."

"It doesn't matter now. I was just hoping my sons' marriages would be different."

CHAPTER TWENTY-EIGHT

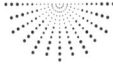

*W*hat would have been Garret and Monica's first wedding anniversary came and went with little notice. The divorce was finalized months earlier, and several weeks before that, Monica moved from Coulson. While Garret put his unfortunate marriage behind him, the tension between him and his father lingered.

In December of 1970, Richard Nixon was preparing to start his third year as president of the United States. American military personnel continued to die in Vietnam, and Tommy, Ryan, and Russell were in their first year of college. Russell was at Harvard while his two childhood friends attended state college.

IT WAS CHRISTMAS EVE AND THEY REACHED COULSON AN hour later than they had originally estimated, due to a traffic accident on the highway. Driving in Tommy's Volkswagen bug, Tommy and Ryan were anxious to get home for Christmas break.

"So you didn't hear from Russell?" Ryan asked as they pulled into Coulson.

"I called and left a message, but I never heard from him," Tommy explained.

"I'll call his parents' place when we get in town, see if he's home for Christmas. Can't believe he wouldn't come home."

"Speak of the devil!" Tommy called out a moment later. He switched lanes and started following a Cadillac; it was pulling into a convenience store parking lot.

"Is that the Coulsons' Caddy?" Ryan asked. It was impossible to see who was driving the car, considering the distance and darkness. The Cadillac had passed them a moment earlier.

"That was Russell," Tommy explained. He drove the Volkswagen into the parking lot and pulled up next to the Cadillac, which had just parked and turned off its engine.

"Hey, Russell!" Tommy and Ryan cried out in unison as they quickly got out of the Volkswagen. Russell, who had just exited the driver's side of his mother's Cadillac, looked more embarrassed than surprised to see his old friends.

Tommy and Ryan paid little attention to Russell's reserve, each excited over the happy coincidence of running into him when first getting into town. They each took turns giving him a welcome hug.

A young woman stepped from the passenger side of the Cadillac and walked to Russell, who was no longer receiving hugs. Possessively, she latched onto Russell's right arm. Instead of eying the strangers with curiosity, she looked impatient to be on her way.

Tommy and Ryan smiled at the beautiful blond woman. While she looked about their age, her aura of sophistication placed her in a class beyond the girls from Coulson. Aside from her striking good looks, Tommy immediately noticed the fur jacket she wore. Silently, he was grateful his kid sister, Katie, wasn't with him, or about now she would be tearing into the girl for wearing the skins of poor dead animals.

"This is Alicia," Russell introduced. "Alicia, this is Tommy and Ryan. We all went to high school together."

Instead of a verbal greeting, Alicia gave Tommy and Ryan a nod and smile, then looked up and said, "Russell, we promised your mother we wouldn't be long."

Russell shifted restlessly, smiled at Alicia then looked at his old friends. "She's right. We did tell my mother we'd be right back."

"I left you a message." Ryan ignored Russell's apparent attempt to cut the meeting short.

"Yeah, I'm sorry. It's been really crazy. How do you guys like school? How is it working out being roommates?" Russell asked.

"I haven't killed him yet." Ryan laughed. Tommy punched Ryan's arm in response.

"Hey, when do you want to get together? How long will you be in Coulson?" Tommy asked.

"Russell," Alicia said in a low, curt tone.

Russell glanced at Alicia, then looked sheepishly at Tommy and Ryan. "Sorry, guys, I really do need to hurry."

"So when do you want to get together?" Ryan repeated Tommy's question.

"I would love to, but Mother seems to have plans for every day I'm home. It was great seeing you, but I need to get going. Merry Christmas!" Not waiting for a response, Russell and Alicia turned from them and walked away.

"Well, fuck, what was that all about?" Tommy asked

after Russell and Alicia disappeared into the convenience store.

"Hell if I know."

THE DAY AFTER CHRISTMAS, ALEXANDRA WAITED IMPATIENTLY for Jimmy to install her new eight-track tape player in her battered red Corvair van. Alexandra, her dark hair pulled into two long pigtails, peered into the vehicle's side window, watching. She wore lavender bellbottom pants that hugged her hips instead of her waist and a paisley print halter top.

Katie sat nearby on the sidewalk, going through a small stack of eight-track tapes her sister had received for Christmas. Katie's moccasin-clad feet peeked out from the tattered cuffs of her denim bellbottoms. Her colorfully embroidered peasant shirt was one size too large for her petite figure, yet the loose fit didn't seem to trouble her.

"This is so cool," Katie said as she read the label of the Creedence Clearwater Revival tape. "I can't wait until I get my license."

"When Jimmy gets it hooked up, we're driving out to Sutter's Lake to meet some friends. Wanna go?"

"Are you going to invite Ryan and Tommy?" Katie glanced to her house, where her brother and Ryan were.

"Why? I'm sure they're going to hook up with their own friends," Alex said.

"Well, I just figured since they're home for Christmas break, we could hang out."

"I don't care." Alex shrugged.

"I wonder why Russell hasn't come over. I figured he'd be here today," Katie said.

"Who knows?" Alex added, "I heard them mention

something about Russell bringing a girlfriend home for Christmas."

"Your sister Alex is looking hot." Ryan stood at Tommy's bedroom window, looking out toward the driveway.

"She's my sister."

"Yeah, so you keep reminding me. But don't worry; I'm not into jailbait."

"Probably a good thing, I have a feeling Jimmy would be pissed if you started hitting on his girlfriend." Tommy sat on his bed, holding a guitar, attempting to tune the instrument.

"According to Jimmy, they're just good friends. Why, has Alex said something different?"

"No. I just figured the kid is always hanging around her. I know if I was spending my Christmas vacation hooking up some girl's tape player, she'd be more than a friend."

"Why do you get pissed when I make cracks about your kid sister, but you're okay with the possibility my brother is hitting on her?" Ryan turned from the window and sat on the floor.

"Probably because I don't worry about Jimmy. I don't think he's a match for Alex."

"Not sure how I feel about that." Ryan laughed. "But you're probably right."

"Did Russell ever call you?"

"No. You?"

"No. I guess he has more important things to do than hang out with old friends."

"Yeah, well, he is a *Harvard* boy now," Ryan said in his best New England accent.

GARRET COULSON SILENTLY OBSERVED THE INTERACTIONS OF his family. The day after Christmas, they were gathered in the living room of Coulson House while Gladys served an informal brunch. He watched as his mother congratulated Russell on his new girlfriend.

"She's a lovely young woman. I'm so pleased she could spend Christmas with us," Vera told Russell.

"Fine family, excellent connections," Randall had mentioned when Alicia was out of earshot. He slapped Russell on the back, congratulating his grandson for his wise choice.

Even Harrison Junior seemed to find Alicia an acceptable match, although his comments were primarily whispered to his younger brothers when no one was listening, something along the lines of, "I bet she'd be a hot little fuck. Have you done her yet?"

Of course, Sonny boy didn't dare voice such crude praise when his own fiancée, Shelly, or his parents or grandfather might overhear his comments. The three elders were equally charmed with Shelly.

Garret could not stomach Alicia or Shelly. In his opinion, both women were spoiled, self-centered, and shallow. He prayed Russell would come to his senses. Since it was only his first year of college, there was hope. What made him nervous was how his parents encouraged the match and would probably be delighted if Russell married the girl before finishing college.

He rather hoped his older brother married Shelly. It would serve him right. But if both women became his sister-in-laws, he didn't imagine future family gatherings would be pleasant. Garret suspected that if Alicia and Shelly were put together in the same room for a prolonged amount of time, they would start sharpening their claws—probably on each other.

"ARENʼT YOU GOING TO SEE SOME OF YOUR FRIENDS WHILE you're in town?" Garret asked Russell when the two were standing together at the edge of the living room, having a private conversation.

"Not really any time. You know Mother."

"True, she loves to plan her little parties. But you always found time for your friends before. Just surprised me, since this is your first time back in Coulson, and you'll only be here for a few days."

"I just don't have time. And I realized a while back, people change and move on. My life's different now, and I don't really have anything in common with my old friends." Russell sipped his mimosa.

"What about your history with them?" Garret asked.

"A person can only spend so much time talking about the good old days."

"Does this mean you aren't moving back to Coulson after graduation?"

"That's quite a ways down the road. And don't forget, I may not be as lucky as you when they pull my lottery numbers."

"I imagine Grandfather can get you out if you get a low number."

"I wouldn't do that. Dad didn't use Grandfather's connections to get him out of the service."

"Well, like you said, that's a ways down the road. And I hope you don't do something stupid like me."

"What do you mean?" Russell asked.

"Rush into a marriage."

"Garret, your marriage, well, that was an entirely different thing. I'm in love with Alicia."

"How do you know? You've only known her for, what, four months, if that?"

"Mother and Dad seem to like her a lot. So does Grandfather."

"Please, Russell, don't rush into anything. Finish college and then think about marriage, if that's what you want to do."

CHAPTER TWENTY-NINE

*B*arreling down the dirt road, windows open, and the music of Simon and Garfunkel blaring from the speakers, Alex steered her van toward Sutter's Lake while Jimmy sat in the passenger seat. Katie sat in the backseat, looking out the window while tapping her hand against her knee in rhythm to the music. Unseasonably warm for December in Coulson, there was no need for jackets.

Tommy and Ryan had already left the house by the time Jimmy was finished installing the tape deck, so Alex didn't invite them to come. She doubted Tommy would be interested, considering they didn't run with the same crowd, and Alex's friends were all in high school.

Once they reached the lake, it didn't take them long to find the campground with their friends. Someone had already started a campfire and was roasting marshmallows when they pulled up and parked. Without taking an actual head count, Alex guessed about twenty of her friends had shown up.

Getting out of the van, she was greeted by Mickey Davidson, a boy she had been seeing for several weeks. Without hesitation, he pulled her into an embrace for a kiss, pressing her back against the vehicle. Wrapping her arms around his neck, Alex pulled him closer and returned the kiss with equal fervor.

Jimmy stepped from the van and paid little attention to his old friend, who was busy exchanging gropes with her current boyfriend. Spotting a girl he had been wanting to ask out, he smiled and walked in the girl's direction. Katie slipped from the van and casually walked past her sister, who was still kissing Mickey.

When the kiss finally ended, Mickey and Alex walked hand in hand to the campfire, where Katie and Jimmy were sitting with friends. Mickey sat on a camp chair while Alex sat on his lap.

"Hey, Alex," Katie said. "Want to hike up to the caves later?"

"I started walking up there when I first got here," Mickey said, "but the paths are all wiped out."

"I bet it was from that rainstorm last week," Jimmy suggested.

"What do you mean? That was just a sprinkle," Alex said.

"Not on our side of town, and I heard Sutter's Lake got hit pretty hard," Jimmy explained. It wasn't unusual to hear about pockets of rain hitting one area of Coulson hard while it remained dry across town.

"Well, I'm game for a hike. We've been up in these hills enough times to be able to find our way by landmarks," Alex said.

After a considerable amount of discussion, it turned out only six people from the group were up to a hike, which included Alex, Jimmy, Mickey, and Katie. The other two hikers were Jane Hilton—the girl Jimmy had his eye on—and Stanley Fields—a junior who had his eye on Katie. Before heading out, the girls visited the public restrooms then met the boys on the path leading to the caves.

"Must have been one hell of a river," Alex commented as she stepped over a tree limb blocking the washed-out pathway. She wasn't wearing a watch, but judging by the location of the sun and the time they had left her house, she guessed it was around 2 p.m. A little breezy, she was beginning to regret not bringing a jacket.

"Shit, there must have been a hell of a lot of water coming through here." Mickey surveyed the area while stepping over storm-placed debris.

Alex glanced over her shoulder and smiled. Trailing behind them were Jimmy and Jane. Jimmy was obviously making a play for Jane, and by the girl's flirtatious smile, it looked as if she was interested. Katie, being high energy, had raced ahead, with Stanley by her side. Considering the time of year, Alex wasn't worried about stumbling over a rattlesnake. The area had mountain lions, but she'd never known of anyone who'd actually seen one of the elusive wild cats in the area.

They had been hiking for about fifteen minutes when Alex heard it—a piercing scream coming from her little sister, Katie. Without hesitation, Alex and Jimmy took off in a full run, dodging fallen tree limbs and misplaced boulders as they made their way to Alexandra's little sister. Jane and Mickey sprinted after them.

The sound of Katie's scream drifted to the campsite, and moments later the rest of the group raced toward what appeared to be a cry for help. When they arrived, they found the six hikers standing a considerable distance from what had once been the hiking trail. Katie and Stanley had wandered off from the pathway, bringing them to what had provoked Katie's outburst.

It didn't take long for the newly arriving teenagers to see what had prompted the scream or what now held the mute attention of the six hikers. Running water had moved the dirt covering what had obviously been a shallow grave. Visible to the teenagers was the skeletal remains of a man, if one was to judge by the tattered suit it wore.

Twenty minutes later, back at the campground, Jimmy used the pay phone to call the police. Alex and Katie returned to the campsite with several others while the rest of the group stayed by the grave site until the authorities arrived. Katie, still shaken from stumbling upon the horrific discovery, allowed Stanley to comfort her. They sat atop a picnic table, observing the activity from a distance. While the gravesite was out of their view, they watched as police vehicles arrived and parked nearby.

Not long after the arrival of the police, the rest of their group returned to the campsite, chased away from the gravesite by the authorities. Instead of going home, the teenagers watched from a safe distance, each speculating on who the corpse might be.

"Shit, I bet it's that guy who stayed at our motel," Jimmy said.

"What guy?" Katie asked.

"They pulled his car from the lake. Remember, when Mike drowned," Jimmy said.

"I remember that," Alex said. "You mentioned the guy had stayed at the motel."

"Yeah, I don't really remember much about him. Other than he used to give Ryan and me candy for not bugging him."

"Who was he?" Katie asked.

"According to Dad, they thought he was a hit man," Jimmy said.

RANDALL COULSON HUNG UP THE PHONE'S RECEIVER. HE looked across the desk to John Weber, who had been sitting silently listening to Randall's side of the conversation. Earlier that afternoon, Randall told his family he was going to his office to get some work done. No one reminded him it was the day after Christmas.

"That was the chief," Randall explained, picking up his cigar.

"So I gathered."

"Looks like last week's rain did more damage than we bargained for."

"What are you going to do?"

"I wouldn't be surprised if those two FBI guys show up again." Randall puffed on his cigar.

"Did they ever talk to Vera?" John asked.

"No. And now that you mention it, they never talked to Sonny either. You still have that photo of Marino?"

"Yes."

"Give it to me. And then destroy any files you have on that son of a bitch."

WITHIN AN HOUR, RANDALL COULSON WAS BACK AT COULSON House and alone in the library, waiting for his eldest grandson.

"They said you wanted to talk to me?" Sonny asked as he

and Shelly walked into the room. Randall looked up from the desk.

"Shelly, if you don't mind, I need to speak to my grandson alone for a moment. It's family business. I won't keep him long."

"Certainly." Shelly flashed a smile at Randall then gave Sonny a quick kiss on the cheek before leaving the room, closing the door behind her. Sonny walked to his grandfather and sat down.

"Sonny, do you remember this man?" Randall handed Sonny a photograph of Anthony Marino. Holding it, Sonny studied the picture carefully and frowned. Randall was the only member of the family who sometimes called Harrison Junior by his childhood nickname.

"No, who is it?" Sonny set the photograph on the desk.

"You met him before you left for Europe. We were having dinner at the Roseville and he sent over a bottle of champagne to our table."

Sonny picked up the photograph again and after a moment smiled.

"That's right, the man who flirted with Mother up at Clement Falls. I remember."

Randall sighed and took back the photograph. He looked up at his grandson.

"Harrison," Randall began, "I want you to listen very carefully to me. It's possible someone from the FBI will want to interview you regarding this man. I don't want you to remember anything beyond the bottle of champagne he sent to the table. I don't want you to say anything to them—or anyone, including Shelly—about the man flirting with your mother. Do you understand?"

"Why?" Sonny asked with a frown.

"That doesn't matter. The less you know, the better. As

far as you're concerned, you remember he sent a bottle of champagne over to our table, but you can't remember anything about the conversation because your thoughts were on your upcoming Europe trip. Do you understand?"

"I don't really understand. But sure, I won't say anything about him flirting with Mother. To be honest, I vaguely remember the guy."

"Good." Randall stood up and walked to the fireplace in the library. He tossed the photograph of Anthony Marino into the flames and watched it burn until there was nothing left but crumbling ashes.

"WHAT IS THIS ABOUT, HARRISON?" VERA ASKED AS SHE walked into her bedroom. Ten minutes earlier, while in the sunroom visiting with Shelly, her husband had whispered to her that she needed to come upstairs immediately, alone. She suspected something strange was going on. First Shelly told her Randall returned home and wanted to speak to Sonny alone, then Harrison was summoned to the library for a private chat with his father.

"Shut the door, please," Harrison told her as he paced the room.

Looking curiously at her husband, she shut the door then walked toward him.

"It's about Anthony Marino," Harrison explained.

Looking as if someone had punched her in the stomach, Vera sat on the wicker chair next to her bed and looked up at Harrison. "Did he come back?"

"In a matter of speaking." He stopped pacing and faced Vera. "Some teenagers found what was left of him buried in a shallow grave not far from where they found his car."

"Are they sure it's him?"

"They just found the body about an hour or so ago, so I don't imagine they're certain of anything at this point. His wallet was with the body, and according to the identification, it's Marino. I imagine they'll run some sort of tests to verify the remains are his."

"But how can we be sure it's him?" Vera's eyes filled with tears.

"Vera," Harrison snapped, "it's him."

Vera's eyes widened, and she stared at her husband. She didn't respond immediately.

"What do you want me to do?" she finally asked.

Harrison sat on the side of the bed next to the wicker chair. Reaching out, he took Vera's hands in his and held them as he looked into her eyes.

"It's possible the FBI might decide to start asking more questions, and that note he gave to Russell could come up again. You weren't here the last time, but if they start asking questions again, I have a feeling they'll want to talk to you."

"What do you want me to say?"

Harrison could feel her trembling as he held her hands. "Stick to the story that you met Marino only once, at the restaurant when he sent the champagne over."

"If they ask why he sent the champagne over, what do I say?"

"That he was trying to ingratiate himself to our family. Tell them you tore the note up after I found it. If they ask about why you left town, repeat the story that you fell in our driveway and injured your ankle and then went to the private clinic for treatment."

"But what if someone remembers seeing me talking to him at Clement Falls...and the one time I talked to him on Main Street?"

Harrison considered her question a moment before answering.

"If they happen to come across someone who remembers seeing you talking to him, don't act overly concerned. Brush it off by saying something like you don't remember seeing him before, but that it is always possible you'd passed him on the street. I know strangers have asked me for directions before, and I couldn't tell you what they looked like the next day."

"Thank you, Harrison." Vera gave him a sad smile.

"Thank you?" Harrison frowned, uncertain what she was thanking him for.

Vera leaned forward and brushed the side of his face with her right hand. "For taking care of me. In spite of all that I've done, you've always been there when I needed you." Vera leaned closer and brushed a kiss over Harrison's lips.

Resting her forehead briefly on his, they closed their eyes and said nothing.

CHAPTER THIRTY

*R*ussell was in the sunroom, saying his final goodbyes to his family before leaving for the airport with Alicia, when Gladys announced two agents from the FBI were here to see them.

"That was quick," Randall muttered under his breath.

"Who do they wish to see?" Garret asked. All the members of the Coulson clan were gathered in the sunroom, including Shelly.

"I'm not really sure, sir. They told me they needed to speak to Mr. Coulson, and when I asked which Mr. Coulson, they said all of them."

"Show them in," Randall told her.

A few moments later Gladys brought the two men into the room. It was Agents Carmichael and Stephens. Harrison and Randall recognized the men.

"It's been a few years," Randall greeted them, putting out his hand first to Carmichael and then to Stephens. "I understand you found your missing hit man."

"I know it was in this morning's newspaper, but there

was no mention about the body's identity," Carmichael commented, eyeing Randall with suspicion.

Randall chuckled and sat back down in his chair. "True, but the police chief called me when they found him. Of course, it could be someone else, despite the fact he had Marino's wallet on him."

Stephens almost asked *why would the police chief call you about the body?* But then he caught himself. It was a foolish question. One thing he and Carmichael had discovered since coming to Coulson ten years earlier was that Randall Coulson owned the town and the police chief.

"Is this about that body that was found by the lake yesterday?" Garret asked.

"What body?" Shelly gasped.

"It was in this morning's newspaper," Russell explained.

"I didn't read the newspaper," Shelly told him.

"So who was he?" Garret asked, now curious.

"And you are?" Carmichael asked.

"This is my son Garret. Garret, this is Agents Carmichael and Stephens. They're with the FBI." The men shook hands as Harrison made the introductions around the room. When he got to Russell, Harrison added, "And my son Russell, you've already met. Although I don't imagine he is as you remember."

"Now I'm feeling old." Carmichael chuckled as he shook Russell's hand.

"I still don't understand. What is this about?" Garret asked after introductions were made.

"It's about this man." Agent Stephens reached into his coat pocket and pulled out a photograph of Anthony Marino. He handed it to Garret.

"Is this the guy they found?" Garret asked.

"We believe so," Stephens said.

"Hey, I know this guy," Garret said. All eyes shifted to Garret. Vera glanced warily to her husband but said nothing.

"You know him?" Stephens asked,

"Well, not really." Garret chuckled. "I suppose the statute of limitations has expired, so no reason to keep it a secret." He handed the photograph back to Stephens, who was clearly intrigued about what Garret had to say.

When Garret glanced up after handing the photograph back to Stephens, he noticed everyone was staring at him.

"He bought me booze," Garret said with a shrug.

"Excuse me?" Carmichael asked.

"I must have been sixteen. Met him in the parking lot of the liquor store and he offered to buy me and my friends some beer and wine. I remember him because when I tried to pay him for buying it, he wouldn't take my money. I paid for the booze, of course, but he wouldn't take anything extra. He even told me where he was staying, and if I ever needed someone to buy, just let him know."

"Did you ever go to his motel room?" Carmichael asked.

"No. Never saw him again. So what's the deal with this guy? My grandfather said something about a hit man?" Garret didn't notice the relief on his mother's face, yet Agent Stephens did.

"That's why we were originally looking for him. We believe he was involved with a hit in Reno. But now we're trying to find out who killed him," Stephens explained.

"Can I see his photograph?" Sonny asked. Stephens handed Sonny the picture.

Randall watched as his eldest grandson looked at the picture then handed it to Russell.

"I understand you met Marino," Carmichael directed his question to Sonny.

"I did?" Sonny frowned, then snatched the picture from Russell and took a second look. He shook his head as if he didn't remember.

"Your father told me you were at a restaurant having dinner and this man sent over a bottle of champagne to your table. This would have been back in October 1960," Carmichael explained while he eyed Sonny curiously.

"I can only remember that happening once when we were at the Roseville. Might have been him. Right time, a week or so before I left for Europe. But I don't really remember him, sorry."

"Do you remember what he talked about when he came to your table?" Carmichael asked.

"I barely remember him. Sorry. I do remember I was pretty excited about going to Europe, so if he had some conversation with my parents or grandfather that night, you probably should ask them. I barely remember the champagne."

"Perhaps we could speak privately with Mrs. Coulson," Stephens asked.

"Me, why?" Vera frowned.

"I just think it might be more comfortable for you if we do this in private," Stephens explained.

Harrison started to object, but Vera reached out and grabbed his hand, giving it a gentle squeeze.

"It's all right, dear. Let me go answer the gentlemen's questions, and then we can finish saying goodbye to Russell." She turned to face the agents. "I trust this won't take long, my son is leaving in a few minutes, and I don't imagine I'll see him again for a few months."

Instead of leaving the sunroom, all but Vera and the agents moved to the living room.

"Can you tell us about the note your son brought you from Marino," Carmichael asked.

"It just said he could get me a great deal on a pair of diamond cufflinks for my husband."

"And why would he have offered to get you a deal on cufflinks?" Carmichael asked.

"I assume for the same reason he sent over the champagne. He wanted to ingratiate himself to my husband and father-in-law."

"But if he wanted to do that, why would he send a private note to the wife and daughter-in-law of the men he wanted to ingratiate himself with? I would imagine that might anger most men, having a stranger send a note to his wife."

Vera smiled sweetly. "I've found people often go out of their way to be nice to me, believing in some way I'll then influence my husband in their favor. It's really not that uncommon. And I'll confess the offer intrigued me. Of course, Harrison found the note that afternoon and pointed out the cufflinks would probably be stolen merchandise. I felt a little foolish and tore up the note."

"And you had never met Marino before? Or saw him after he sent over the champagne?"

"No, never." Vera continued to smile.

"I understand you hurt your ankle about this time. From what I recall, you were gone when we came to interview your youngest son."

"Yes, I was."

"I assume you saw a doctor before you left?" Stephens asked.

"Yes, I did. Dr. Phillips, he came to the house. He was such a dear man."

"Was?" Carmichael asked.

"Dr. Phillips passed away about five years ago." Vera continued to smile sweetly.

"Where did you say you went for the therapy treatment for your ankle?" Stephens asked.

"Oh, I really don't recall the name of the clinic. It was so long ago. But you can ask my husband."

"WHAT'S WITH ALL THE QUESTIONS ABOUT THE ANKLE?" Carmichael asked as the two agents walked to their car.

"I guess you missed it. But when the middle son said something about knowing the guy, you should have seen his mother's expression. What really got me was her look of relief after he told his story."

"From what I've learned about the family, he's been the wild one. Maybe she was afraid he'd gotten involved with the guy back then."

"I don't think that's it."

Both men got into a dark sedan and closed the doors. Carmichael started the engine and began driving down the long, steep driveway leading from Coulson House to the street.

"You think there was something between Mrs. Coulson and Marino?" Carmichael asked.

"When we looked into the Coulsons ten years ago, it didn't take much to find out they slept in separate bedrooms, and he had a string of mistresses. Knowing Marino, someone like Vera Coulson would catch his eye, especially if he thought she was a neglected wife."

"So why send champagne to their table?"

"The same reason he loved to taunt us after a hit. But you know what I find interesting?"

"What?"

"I find it interesting Vera Coulson used the same word as her husband did when we originally interviewed him. Both she and her husband said Marino was trying to *ingratiate* himself to them."

"You think she was coached?" Carmichael asked.

"What do you think?"

"Well, what I found interesting was that Harrison Coulson remembered our names after all these years."

"I gave the maid a business card when she answered the door," Stephens reminded him.

"Didn't you notice? She looked at the card and then set it on a table in the entry. She didn't take the card with her. Plus, you gave her your business card, not mine. I guess this means we should have looked closer after they found the car." Carmichael sighed.

"We both thought there was a possibility Marino dumped his own car in the lake."

"I know."

"I just wish we could talk to Vera Coulson's doctor."

"Yeah, like he would really talk to us even if he was still alive." Carmichael snorted.

"I'd like to know what clinic she stayed at, and if it was really for a broken ankle," Stephens said.

"Why, what are you thinking?" Carmichael asked.

"Marino had a history of smacking around his women. We know he probably killed his second wife and her lover, and his last wife disappeared with his kid. She was tired of being a punching bag. Maybe Mrs. Coulson got in a little too deep and her husband or father-in-law cleaned up her mess."

"I suppose that's possible, but we have absolutely no proof, and if we go snooping around or trying to check out the clinic, it'll be our asses. Old man Coulson has some pretty influential friends in Washington."

"I know." Stephens sighed and looked out the car's side window, watching the Coulson landscape roll by. "And I suppose whoever iced Marino did us all a favor. Although for curiosity's sake, I would love to know what happened."

"Well, we have one more stop," Carmichael reminded him.

"You want to go now?"

"Might as well, then we can wrap this up and head home."

SOMEONE WAS RINGING HIS DOORBELL. HE WONDERED BRIEFLY if his daughter had forgotten her key. She had gone down the street earlier to see what Santa had brought her best friend. Opening the front door, it wasn't his daughter but two young men wearing gray business suits. Those who visited him this time of year normally wore jeans and parkas.

Glancing past the men, he noted the sky over Clement Falls was clear, yet there were still some patches of snow on the ground.

"Nick Carracci?" one of the men said. Nick squinted; he'd forgotten to put on his glasses. The men looked familiar.

"Yes," Nick answered.

"Hello, I'm Agent Carmichael and this is Agent Stephens —" Before Agent Carmichael finished saying his name, Nick remembered. It was those G-men looking for his brother-in-law.

"I know who you are," Nick interrupted the introductions.

"Do you think we could talk inside?" Carmichael shivered. "It's pretty cold out here."

Nick didn't answer immediately. Finally, he opened the door wider so the two men could walk in. He showed them to the parlor, where they each took a seat.

"I believe we found your brother-in-law," Carmichael told him.

"I wondered if it was Anthony. When I read the article in the newspaper about them finding a body near the area where they found his car, I thought it might be him."

"We haven't made a positive ID yet."

"So why are you here?" Nick asked.

"The last time we were up here and spoke to your wife —" Carmichael began.

"My wife died," Nick interrupted. He remembered their last visit, when they had interviewed him and Gina. While she wanted them to find her brother, there was much she wouldn't tell them. Nick didn't want to upset his wife; her health was failing, so he had said little.

"Yes, we understand, and we're sorry for your loss. But we hoped that perhaps you might have remembered something about your brother-in-law's last visit that you forgot to tell us before. I remember your wife was quite upset he was missing, but she told us very little about his visit here or if he had any friends locally."

"I never liked my brother-in-law, but Gina loved her brother. I have to admit he was always very good to her. But I saw how he treated his wife, and I heard stories. I didn't trust his friends."

"He had friends here?" Stephens asked.

"No, back where we came from. He didn't have any friends here, not that I know of."

"Why was he visiting you?" Carmichael asked.

"Gina said he was just here to see her, but I overheard them talking. He told her he had to lie low for a while, that he'd pissed someone off back home, but he promised her it would blow over."

"Why would he have told her anything?" Stephens asked.

"She still had friends back home who she kept in touch with. He didn't want her to say anything about his visit when she talked to them."

"Why did he leave Clement Falls? Why move down to Coulson and rent a room?" Carmichael asked.

"He told me he didn't want to deal with the snow. It was October when he left, and we normally start getting snow in December, sometimes November."

"And what did he tell his sister?" Stephens asked.

Nick considered the question for a minute.

"Nick, you didn't see how he looked at her, Mrs. Coulson," Gina had told him after her brother left the mountain. *"He's going to get himself in trouble, I know it."*

"I think he was bored at Clement Falls. There isn't much to do up here, and he figured he could lie low in Coulson as well as here." Nick didn't lie; he just didn't see a reason to drag an important woman like Mrs. Coulson into his brother-in-law's mess.

"So he never mentioned to you or your sister anyone he knew or wanted to get to know. A woman perhaps?"

Nick didn't answer immediately; he just stared at the two agents. Finally, he answered.

"No. He never mentioned anyone."

BACK IN THEIR VEHICLE, CARMICHAEL AND STEPHENS HEADED down off the mountain.

"We really don't have anything to support a connection between Vera Coulson and Anthony Marino. If you think about it, all we have is Marino sending champagne, Marino sending a note. We have absolutely nothing to indicate the Coulsons initiated or encouraged a relationship with the man. Aside from an unused condom Keller threw away, we don't even know if Marino was seeing any woman," Carmichael said.

"I suppose you're right. We haven't interviewed a single person who claims to have seen Marino even talking with any of the Coulsons. The most logical conclusion, Marino didn't lie low enough, and his past caught up with him."

CHAPTER THIRTY-ONE

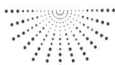

*B*y the second week of the New Year 1971, Ryan and Tommy had returned to the dorm at the state college, and Russell was back at Harvard. Sonny and Shelly had gone home to Chicago, where Sonny worked at Coulson Enterprises' Chicago division. Although Sonny continued to have limited responsibilities with the family business, his interview with the FBI agents had impressed his grandfather.

While Harrison Junior possessed no business savvy, Randall began envisioning a different future for his eldest grandson—politics—where Randall pulled the strings. He wondered if it was perhaps time to get Harrison properly wed and back in Coulson.

The story of a reported hit man's body being found up by Sutter's Lake kept the locals buzzing for a few weeks, but by Saint Patrick's Day, Marino was a distant memory. Aside from the Kellers and the Coulsons, no one in town remembered seeing the man. Most assumed he was simply passing through and whoever was responsible for his death was probably someone from Anthony Marino's past, with no connection to Coulson. All assumed the killers were long gone. Even Russell and Garret, who had met the man, had a limited memory of him. Anthony Marino left no lasting impression on either brother.

―――――――

VERA SAT AT HER DRESSING TABLE, BRUSHING HER HAIR BEFORE going to bed, when a knock came at her bedroom door.

"Come in," she called out. Setting the brush on the marble tabletop, she turned to see who it was. Harrison walked in, closing the door behind him.

"I thought you were going to the club tonight?" Vera asked, surprised to see her husband still at home.

"No, I didn't feel like going. Plus, I wanted to talk to you." He lingered by the closed door.

"Come, please sit down." Vera pointed to the empty wicker chair by her bedside. Picking up her brush, she turned to face the mirror again. Harrison walked over to the wicker chair and sat down. He watched Vera brush her hair. She was still a beautiful woman, much younger looking than her actual years.

"I thought you'd like to know Dad spoke to some friends of his in the bureau."

Vera put the brush down again and turned to face Harrison.

"The FBI?" she asked.

"Yes. They haven't any new leads on Marino's death. They're fairly certain someone from his past was responsible. But with no new leads, they're looking at it as a cold case. It doesn't look as if they plan to put much effort into finding who's responsible."

"Now what?" Vera asked.

"I suppose we go on like we always have," Harrison said.

"I don't know if I can," Vera whispered.

"What do you mean?"

"I know our marriage started off all wrong. And it was my fault."

"That's not true, Vera."

"You didn't want to marry me. That was pretty obvious."

"I was young. So were you. There were things I didn't understand back then, things about you, about myself."

"And you understand now?" she asked.

"Not everything, but yes, I think I understand better now. For a while, after Harrison was born, I thought things were going to work out for us. But then Garret was born and you pushed me away. And after Russell was born, you made it clear you didn't want me in your bed again."

"And you just accepted it?"

"I wasn't going to beg, Vera. Not after all we'd been through."

"But you didn't understand." Vera glanced down, unable to look into her husband's eyes.

"Then explain it to me."

They were silent for a moment.

"After Garret was born," Vera began, "I was just so tired and I couldn't sleep. I felt so guilty because I wasn't happy. I had two healthy boys, but that didn't matter to me. Sometimes...sometimes I just didn't want to live anymore."

"Why didn't you say something?"

"Say what? As it was, your mother thought I was a horrible mother. And after a few months, it got better, and I started feeling like myself again. But then Russell was born, and it was even worse than after Garret's birth."

"In what way?"

"I was so depressed, and when I looked at Russell, I just wanted him to go away. I know that's a horrible thing to admit, but that's how I felt. I didn't feel like eating, I couldn't sleep, and being intimate with you—I couldn't bear the thought. But it wasn't you, Harrison. It was me." Vera looked to the floor for a moment.

"One day..." Vera looked up into Harrison's face. "I have never told anyone this before, and while I don't think Garret remembers, I suspect he remembers something."

"What happened, Vera?"

"Russell was about three months old, and I just couldn't handle his incessant crying. His neediness."

"But he was just three months old."

"I know that." Vera smiled sadly. "But at the time I didn't care. All I wanted was for the pain to stop. I took Russell upstairs to the third floor—to one of the rooms with a balcony. Garret followed us up there, but I didn't realize it at the time.

"I went out onto the balcony with Russell." Vera closed her eyes, visualizing the long ago event. "It was breezy that day. The air felt so good on my face. While holding Russell in my arms, I stepped up onto the ledge of the balcony, fully intending to jump."

"Oh my god." Harrison's face went ashen.

"Garret ran onto the balcony and shouted for me to get down. He was frightened. He was about eight at the time. I held out my hand and asked him to join me. I told him we could fly."

"Good lord," Harrison muttered. He felt ill.

"And then, something pushed me, right off the ledge, back onto the balcony. I don't know how I managed it, but Russell was still safe in my arms. By this time, Garret had run out of the room, terrified, I suppose. And then I saw her."

"You saw who?"

"Your mother. As clear as you sitting there. And then, she vanished. Falling seemed to snap me back to my senses, and I was horrified at what I'd almost done. Not just to me but to our sons. I immediately went to find Garret. I convinced him I was just playing. I told him it was foolish play, and he promised not to say anything."

"My mother?"

"Oh, I don't know. I suppose it was some sort of hallucination. After that, I tried to stay away from Russell...away from Garret. I didn't want to hurt them. By the time Russell was almost a year old, I started feeling normal again. But by that time, I had pushed everyone away; I didn't feel there was any way to repair the damage."

"I've heard about this before, with other women. Did you ever discuss this with the doctor at the sanitarium?"

"No, I was too ashamed. As it was, we discussed our marriage—our courtship. He helped me understand myself a little better. But I couldn't tell him about the thoughts I had about hurting our boys—myself. What type of monster wants to hurt her child?"

"I don't believe you're a monster, Vera. In your own way, you tried to protect them by keeping your distance." He noticed her brushing away tears. "How do you feel about me?"

"What do you mean?" she asked.

"What are your feelings toward me?"

Their eyes met. "I love you, Harrison. I've always been in love with you."

Harrison stood up and walked toward his wife. She

watched silently as he offered her his hand. She accepted it and stood up.

"I don't want to go on as we have. I'd like to have a real marriage," Harrison told her, his voice barely a whisper.

"Do you think that's possible?"

"All we can do is try, Vera...All we can do is try."

CHAPTER THIRTY-TWO

uring the summer of 1971, Coulson Enterprises, in its campaign to boost its public image, purchased new bleachers for the local high school's football field. It was just one of the many philanthropic projects backed by Coulson Enterprises.

Randall Coulson had recently established a nonprofit organization based in Coulson, headed by his eldest grandson, who had recently returned to the community with his new bride, Shelly. At first, Shelly objected to the move, until Randall took her aside and explained the terms of his will.

"Do you like Coulson House?" Randall had asked Sonny's new wife.

"It's amazing," Shelly said. While she wasn't overly impressed with the community of Coulson, she had fallen in love with the magnificent estate.

"Then perhaps you need to be aware of the arrangements I've made. When I die, Coulson House goes to my son. When Harrison passes, the estate goes to his oldest son —or to that son's eldest heir. So someday, Coulson House will belong to your husband. But there's no reason to wait, you can enjoy the estate now and treat it as your own home. If you move back to Coulson, I'll turn over the east wing to you and young Harrison, and someday the entire property will be his."

Wanting to reside in the castle on the hill, Shelly agreed to the move. The one thing she found disappointing was Garret and Russell's apparent disinterest that someday Coulson House would belong to her—and not to them. She couldn't believe her brother-in-laws didn't secretly covet the property.

IN SPITE OF GARRET'S BUSINESS ACUMEN, HE CONTINUED TO BE a reckless spirit. With his grandfather and the Harrisons' attentions turned toward politics, he was pressured to practice some discretion, which he managed to do to some extent. Now a successful and wealthy businessman, Garret seemed incapable of finding contentment in his personal life.

Since he hadn't lived at Coulson House for years, he hadn't observed the subtle changes in his parents' marriage, nor the fact his father now slept in his mother's room each night. Garret continued to carry the baggage of his youth.

RUSSELL RETURNED FOR HOMECOMING IN OCTOBER OF 1971, yet he didn't bring Alicia with him, who was now his fiancée. Randall insisted his youngest grandson make a showing at homecoming with Garret, since they had each graduated from the local high school, and it was a public relations opportunity. Technically speaking, Sonny had not graduated from the local high school but from the original school that had been converted from a K–12 to an elementary school during Garret's junior year.

IT WAS HALFTIME DURING THE HOMECOMING GAME. GARRET and Russell sat next to each other on the crowded football bleachers. Garret glanced at his watch, impatient for the game to commence and eventually end so he could take off. While he enjoyed football, watching a high school game held little appeal. Nor was he especially interested in sitting through the parade of convertibles now making their way between the football field and bleachers.

The cars carried contenders for the homecoming king and queen. Even when he was in high school, he found such pageantry exceedingly boring. When the convertibles stopped, he glanced up and saw her, the contender in the car directly in front of him, not ten feet away.

Startled by his body's physical reaction to the young woman, Garret could just stare. It wasn't an embarrassing bulge in his pants, something that would hardly be politically prudent considering she was just a child, maybe seventeen. The sensation was more like someone had punched him in the gut and he needed to catch his breath. Even so, Garret was uncomfortable with his fascination over a fresh-faced beauty, making him feel a bit like a gawking pervert.

Smiling to the crowd, she turned toward him, but he doubted she was looking at anyone in particular. She was everything he was not—wholesome, innocent, an unspoiled beauty with her entire life ahead of her. He wanted to wrap her up in his arms and protect her.

He nudged Russell. "Who in the hell is that?" Garret

nodded to the brunette in the first car, her long hair cascading down her back.

"Alex Chamberlain, you know, her mom was your algebra teacher."

"Holy shit. I certainly was right." Garret smiled, wishing he were ten years younger.

"Right about what?"

"She's a heartbreaker." Garret had no way of knowing that in fourteen years the heart she would be breaking was his.

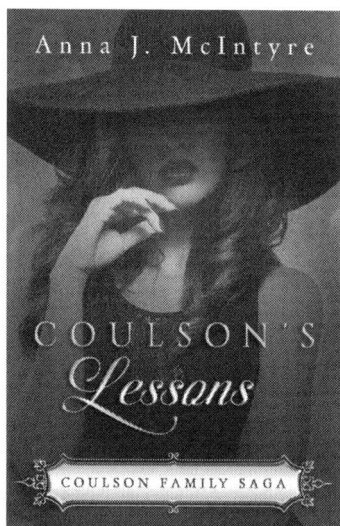

Anna J. McIntyre

COULSON'S
Lessons

COULSON FAMILY SAGA

RETURN TO COULSON IN

COULSON'S LESSONS

After losing her beloved husband in a car accident, Alexandra is left to raise her teenage son alone. Coming to terms with life as a single mother is difficult enough, yet now she must face the sins of her past when Garret Coulson returns to town.

Grandson of the town's founder, the wealthy and powerful Garret Coulson fell in love with another man's wife, resulting in a self-imposed exile. With that man dead, Garret can return to claim what should have been his.

For ten years, Alexandra has kept the secret of her infidelity. The fact she is now a widow does not make that secret any less painful to reveal. Some secrets have the power to shatter lives—yet sometimes they heal hearts.

BOOKS BY ANNA J. MCINTYRE

COULSON FAMILY SAGA

Coulson's Wife

Coulson's Crucible

Coulson's Lessons

Coulson's Secret

Coulson's Reckoning

Unlocked Hearts

Sundered Hearts

After Sundown

While Snowbound

Sugar Rush

BOOKS BY BOBBI HOLMES

HAUNTING DANIELLE

NON-FICTION BOOKS

BY BOBBI ANN JOHNSON HOLMES

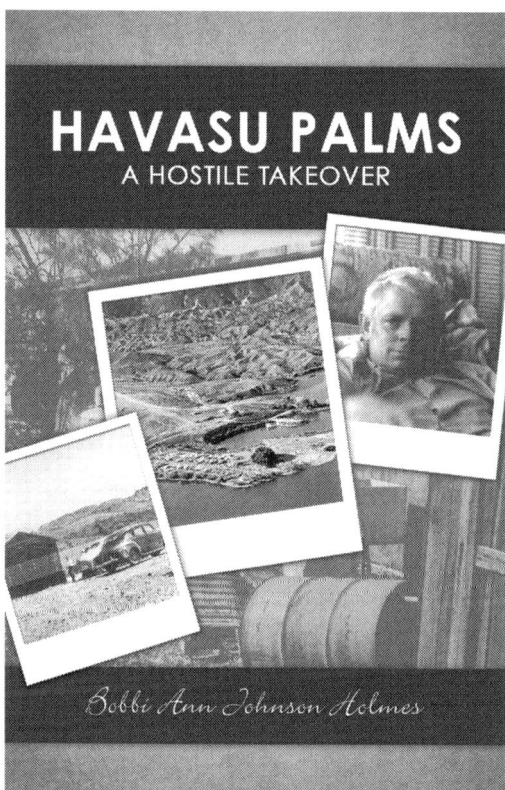

HAVASU PALMS, A HOSTILE TAKEOVER

WHERE THE ROAD ENDS, HAVASU PALMS RECIPES & REMEMBRANCES

MOTHERHOOD, A BOOK OF POETRY

Printed in Great Britain
by Amazon

44078918R00151